I started crawling on my belly up the stairs. I didn't have much strength left. I hated the beast for what he'd done to my brother and to my wife and daughter. And yet no matter how much I hated him, I hated Reeves even more.

When I reached the top step, I raised my head and stared deep into the gloom. Reeves was crouched beneath a fancy painting of himself. Next to him crouched the wolf, eyes yellow in the darkness.

Reeves squeezed off several more shots. And then in the sudden silence he whispered low, that same Indian word he had used the first night when the wolf attacked me.

I raised myself and looked directly into the wolf's eyes as he lowered his blood-spattered head and prepared to lunge at me. He was still bleeding from the bullet Annie had put in him.

And then he dove at me, all slashing teeth and furious noise. . . .

WOLF MOON

Ed Gorman

FAWCETT GOLD MEDAL • NEW YORK

A Fawcett Gold Medal Book
Published by Ballantine Books
Copyright © 1993 by Ed Gorman

All rights reserved under International and Pan-American Copyright Conventions. Published in the United States by Ballantine Books, a division of Random House, Inc., New York, and simultaneously in Canada by Random House of Canada Limited, Toronto.

Library of Congress Catalog Card Number: 93–90087

ISBN 0-449-14836-X

Manufactured in the United States of America

First Edition: June 1993

To Bernie Nalaboff,
this folk tale

"I had looked into wild animal eyes only from a distance. And there had been something in those eyes that was not to be found in the eyes of my fellow humans. They were eyes that looked at me from the other side of the universe . . . separated from me by a gulf neither man nor beast could cross."

—Gordon R. Dickson, *Time Storm*

Thanks to Nancy Hamilton for helping make this novel historically accurate. Any mistakes are mine.

—EG

The wolves lived on a perch high in the mountains so that the leader of the pack could see anything that threatened his mate or their pups. Behind the perch was a cave that served as a den. It was a shared responsibility to bring their pups food. It was not easy. The land was filled with two-legs and their guns. That was why they lived so high up, near where the jagged peaks touched the clouds.

Of course, the wolf knew that man was a devious foe. He did not always show himself when he meant to destroy the wolves.

The leader remembered last spring, when four of the pups had wandered off to hunt and had found for themselves a piece of buffalo meat that a rancher had poisoned with strychnine. The pups had died long and terrible deaths cuddled up against the belly of their mother, while she cried for hours into the dark and indifferent night.

Only one pup had lived, and about this last son the leader and his wife were protective to the point of mania. When the pup slept, the leader sat just outside the den, so that nobody could get inside without killing him first. When the pup accompanied the mother on a small hunt, she never once let him stray, despite the wolf ritual of letting the pups wander off and find their own food.

By the time he was six months, and by the time the white and bitter snows came, the pup stood thirty inches high at the shoulder and measured six feet from the tip of his nose to the tip of his tail. An Indian boy with a white man's lasso managed to get the rope over the pup's neck one day but, incredibly, the pup's powerful jaws cleaved the rope with a single bite. The Indian boy ran off, convinced he had encountered a dire and supernatural being.

By the summer, leader and mate began giving their huge and eager pup a little more freedom.

Because of this, the pup was drinking from a winding mountain stream the day he heard the shots from up on the ledge where the den was.

In fear and rage the pup made his way quickly up the shifting rocks of the mountain.

He saw his mother lying dead, her head exploded from several bullets, her limp body hanging over the edge of a promontory.

At this same moment, his father was being held up by his rear paws and a shaggy and filthy man was gutting him with a bowie knife.

The shaggy man saw the pup. "Schroeder, look at that pup!"

For the first time, the pup set eyes on the sleek and handsome human named Schroeder. He was everything the other man was not—well-attired in fancy hunting clothes, well-spoken, composed and radiating a self-confidence that was almost oppressive.

Schroeder turned now and beheld the pup. His face showed true awe as he studied the imposing animal. He said, simply, "I don't care how long it takes you, Greenleaf. I want that pup. Do you understand me?"

2

And so the hunt began.

It took the wolfer known as Greenleaf four days, but finally, with the help of two Indian trackers, he captured the pup and turned him over to Schroeder. His reward was $1,000 cash and a night in a Denver whorehouse with a former slave girl named (by her madam) Esmerelda.

Schroeder never saw Greenleaf again and didn't care. He had the pup. And he had his very special plans for the pup.

1

The first thing I did after leaving the saloon was find an alley and throw up. We'd been two hard days riding and I still hadn't gotten over the killing yet. I had never robbed a bank before, and I had certainly never seen a man die before, either, especially one of my own brothers. The man named Schroeder had killed him without hesitation or mercy.

So tonight I'd had too much to drink, trying to forget how I'd been changed from eighteen-year-old farm boy to bank robber in the course of forty-eight hours. And trying to forget how Glen had looked dying there by the side of the road when we were dividing the money with Schroeder.

After I finished in the alley, I went back to the dusty street. The water wagon had worked most of the afternoon, but by now, near midnight, the dust rose like ghosts from the grave. The eighty-degree temperature didn't make things any more pleasant, either.

The sleeping room Don and I rented was over the livery stable. The owner had built two small rooms up there and put in cots and a can to piss in and fancied himself in the hotel business. He wanted Yankee cash up front and he wanted a promise not to smoke in bed. All the hay in the stalls below would go up like tinder,

4

he said. We wouldn't have put up with his rules, Don and I, but there were no other rooms to be had.

The livery was dark. You could hear the horses talking to themselves in their sleep. The windless air was sweet and suffocating with the aroma of their shit.

I took the outside stairs leading up to the sleeping rooms. Halfway up I heard the moan. I stopped, just standing there, feeling my stomach and bowels do terrible things. Despite the fact that I looked like a big, jovial, sun-baked farm boy, I was given to nerves and the stomach of an old man.

I eased my .45 from my holster.

I'd recognized the moan as belonging to my older brother, Don. You don't grow up with somebody and not know all the sounds he makes.

The night sky was black and starry. The animals below were still jibbering and snorting as they slept. The saloon music was distant now, and lonely in the hot night air.

I started climbing the stairs on tiptoes.

When I got to the landing, I found the door leading to the hall was ajar. I eased it open, gripping my gun tighter.

The shadows were so deep I had the momentary sense of going blind.

He moaned again, Don did, behind the door down the hall and to the right.

I tiptoed over, put my hand on the knob and gave it an inward push.

You could smell the dying on him. The blood and the seeping poisons.

In the pale light of the moon-facing window he lay on his cot as if the undertaker had already done him up. He lay unmoving with his hands folded primly on his belly and his raw, naked feet arranged precisely side

5

by side, sticking straight up in a way that was almost funny.

Then I got foolish, because he was my brother and all, and because my other brother had passed on less than forty-eight hours ago.

I went straight into the room without considering that somebody might be behind the door.

Don moaned just as I reached his cot. I could see the wounds now, deep knife slashes across his neck and chest and arms. At least, I thought they were knife slashes.

The growl came up from the gravelike darkness behind the door. Hearing it, Don made a whimpering dying-animal noise that scared me because I knew he had only minutes to go.

I turned toward the growl and there they stood—a handsome, trim man in a dark suit much too hot for this kind of summer night, and a timber wolf so big and well-muscled he had to go at least 180 pounds. But size wasn't the only thing that made the lobo remarkable. His coat glowed silver—there was no other way to think of it except glowing—and his eyes glowed yellow, the color of a midnight moon.

The animal I'd never seen before. The man was plenty familiar. He was Schroeder, the man who'd hired us to rob the bank he was part owner of. Afterward we were supposed to split the money four ways—three for us brothers, one for Schroeder. But he'd double-crossed us, killing Glen in the process. But we'd been suspicious of Schroeder and had stashed the money under the foundation of a little white country church. It had taken Schroeder a day and a half to figure out that we'd double-crossed him right back.

Now he was here to get the rest of the money.

6

He used a few Indian words I didn't understand. And then the lobo, growling again, sprang.

He went right for my gun hand, teeth tearing into my wrist, knocking my gun to the floor before I could possibly fire a shot.

The lobo then did to me what he'd done to my brother, whose wounds I now knew had been caused by teeth, not a knife.

He came for me then. He was so well-trained he didn't even make much noise. He just worked his slashing teeth and ripping claws over my face and chest and belly.

I wasn't long awake, of course, not with all the pain, not with all the blood.

There was just the lobo, that glowing lunging body, and those haunted glowing eyes. . . .

For a time all I could hear was my own screaming. Then I couldn't hear much of anything at all.

2

Three months later, a judge named Emmanuel Byers sentenced me to twelve years in territorial prison for my part in the bank robbery.

You hear a lot of stories about prison, and most of them, unfortunately, are true. I was put in a steel five-by-seven cell on the south wing. There were two canvas hammocks for sleeping and one chair for sitting. If you took instruction in reading and writing, as I did, you were allowed to keep a book in your cell. I learned to read and write so well that a lady reporter came out one time and wrote a piece about me. She was especially impressed with the fact that I could recite whole chunks of Shakespeare from memory.

Most of the time I did what most prisoners did. I worked at the quarry. The owner paid the warden eighty cents a day per man. The warden, it was said, paid forty cents to the territorial government and kept the rest for himself. This was in the summer. In the winter I worked on the river, cutting and storing ice for the Union Pacific Railroad. The warden had a cousin who was some kind of railroad vice-president, and the cousin was said to pay plenty for us men, with the warden and himself dividing the spoils.

The first man I bunked with was an Indian who had stabbed to death a man he insisted was a Negro. His lawyer eventually got an old Negro woman to swear that the dead man had been colored, which saved the Indian's life. The judge, learning that the victim was only one more shabby black man, called off the Indian's scheduled execution and let him go free after six months.

During all this time, I wrote letters to Gillian, a young woman I'd known my last two years on the farm. Her father had run the general store. She'd been my partner at harvest moon dances and on the sledding hills near Christmas. I loved her, though I'd never been able to quite say that out loud, and she loved me, a sentiment she expressed frequently. The first three or four times I'd written her, she hadn't responded. I imagined she was still upset over the fact that the man she loved was a bank robber, though as I pointed out in those letters, it was Don and Glen who'd been the robbers, I'd just sort of gone along this one time to see what it was like. Also to their credit, as I noted in those same letters, nobody had ever been killed or even shot during any of their robberies. Eventually she started writing back, though she admitted that she had to be careful her father didn't find out. He was a typical townsman in his belief that criminals of any stripe should be hanged and utterly forgotten.

About seven months into my sentence, I got a letter from Gillian with a new address. She said her father had found out about her writing me and had demanded that she stop. She'd refused. And so she was now living in the mountains in a gold-mining town where, after a few weeks, she'd met a dandy named Reeves, a man who reminded her an awful lot of Schroeder, at least as I'd described him. One day this Reeves got his photograph in the local paper. He'd just become co-owner of the town's largest bank. The other owner was a retiring Yankee major named Styles. This Reeves fellow would run everything from now on. The photograph showed that Gillian had good instincts. It was Schroeder himself, back in the banking business under a new name and in a new town. I wondered how long it would take him to arrange a robbery of his new bank.

One day at the quarry a fierce murderer named Maples, a man nobody troubled, not even the guards, started making fun of a fifteen-year-old boy who was serving time for killing his father. The boy was pretty and slender as a girl. It was whispered that Maples was sweet on the boy but that the boy wouldn't oblige him in any way. This day at the quarry Maples suddenly went crazy. For no reason that anybody could see, he grabbed the boy and hurled him into the water. Then Maples, still crazed and angrier than anybody had seen him, ran down into the water himself and grabbed the boy, who was just now getting up, and held the boy down under the water till he drowned. Several times the boy surfaced, screaming and puking, but Maples just kept holding his head under until the deed was done. I started down into the water, but an old con who'd always looked out for me grabbed my arm and whispered, "Maples'll just kill you next, kid, if'n you go down there." And I knew he was right. And so I just stood there like all the other men in that hot dusty quarry and watched one man kill another.

My fourth year there tuberculosis walked up and down the cell blocks. More than two hundred men died in four months.

In all my time inside I had only one fight, when a new man, trying to impress everybody, made fun of my face, how it was all scarred up from the wolf that time. I don't know why it bothered me so much, but it did and I damned near killed him with my fists. For that I got what the guards called a "shower bath," which meant stripping me naked and directing a stream of high pressure water from a hose to my face, chest, and crotch. When you fell down, they kept spraying away, till your balls were numb and your nose and mouth ran with blood. I was so sick with diarrhea afterward, I lost twenty pounds in the next week and a half.

In a way, even though I'd been angry when the warden told me I couldn't grow a beard, I was grateful for how scarred my face was. Sure, people looked away when they first saw me—I was a monster now, not a human being—but my appearance always reminded me of why, lying there in the doc's office right after the white wolf attacked me—why, despite the physical pain from the bites and slashes, and the mental pain of having seen both my brothers die—why I wanted to go on living.

I wanted to repay Schroeder for how he'd betrayed us. That was my one reason for existing.

Parole was not a major event. Early in the morning of a certain day, a guard took me forward to the warden's office, where I received ten dollars, a suggestion that I read every day the Bible the warden had just handed me, and a plea to stay away from bad people like myself. When you wait so many years for something, you expect to feel exuberant. I didn't feel much of anything at all. I just wanted to see Gillian and hear more about Schroeder.

A buggy took me to the train depot, where I sat for an hour on a hard little bench and let the locals gawk at me. It probably wasn't real hard to see that I'd just gotten out of prison.

By the time it was a year and a half old, the wolf was no longer a pup. Nor was it exactly a wolf. Its weight of 160 pounds marked its maturity, but the tasks it performed belonged not to the wolf family—which was essentially peaceful except for hunting—but to a predatory state that could only be man-made.

Schroeder, using methods a wolfer named Briney had shown him, built an enormous cage for the animal and let him out only when there was a task to be performed—or only when the wolf was being trained.

Schroeder believed that violence begat violence, and so he was remarkably cruel with the wolf. When the animal failed to perform properly, Schroeder beat the animal until it crawled and whimpered. Thus broken, it once again became malleable.

Schroeder trained the animal for eight months before testing it.

One chill March day, Schroeder took a husky about the same size as the wolf and put it in the cage, locked the door, and spoke aloud the Indian command for ''kill,'' which was supposed to turn the wolf into a frenzied beast.

The wolf did not turn on the husky.

Schroeder spent an hour alternately calling out the command and threatening the animal.

When it was finally clear that the wolf would not attack the husky, Schroeder opened the cage, withdrew the dog, and then began beating the wolf until the animal seemed ready to turn on its master.

But Schroeder had been ready for that. He clubbed the animal across the skull with a ball bat. The animal collapsed into unconsciousness.

This training continued until the year that Schroeder met the Chase brothers and arranged for them to rob the bank of which he was part owner.

By then the wolf was obedient, as he proved when he murdered the one Chase brother and cruelly attacked the other.

The wolf no longer remembered the smell of smoky autumn winds and the taste of cool clear creek water and the beauty of sunflowers in the lazy yellow sunlight. He no longer even remembered his mother and father.

There was just the cage. There was just his master. There was just the whip. There was just the prey he was sometimes ordered to kill and rend.

He was still called a wolf, of course, by everyone who saw him.

But he was no longer a true wolf at all. He was something more. And something less.

On a fine sunny dawn, the roosters stirring, the wolf awoke to find that he had company in the large cage.

A raccoon had burrowed under the wire and was just now moving without any fear or inhibition toward the wolf.

Instinctively the wolf knew something was wrong with the raccoon. For one thing, such an animal was not very often brave, not around a wolf anyway.

And for another, there was the matter of the raccoon's mouth, and the curious foamy substance that bearded it. Something was very wrong with this raccoon.

It struck before the wolf had time to get to its feet.

It ripped into the wolf's forepaw and brought its jaws tight against the bone.

The wolf cried out in rage and pain, utterly surprised by the speed and savagery with which the raccoon had moved.

In moments the raccoon was dead, trapped in the teeth and jaws of the wolf as it slammed the chunky body of the raccoon again and again against the bars of the cage.

And then the wolf, still enraged, eviscerated it, much as the wolf had been taught to eviscerate humans.

Then it was done.

The wolf went back to his favorite end of the cage and lay down. His forepaw still hurt and he still cried some, but oddly, he was tired, exhausted, and knew he needed sleep.

When he woke, he stared down at the forepaw. A terrible burning had infected it.

He still wondered about the raccoon and where it had gotten all that nerve to come into his cage and attack him.

Soon enough the wolf went back to sleep, the inexplicable drowsiness claiming him once again.

3

In the summer of '98 the folks in Rock Ridge were just starting to sink the poles and string the wire for telephones. I knew this because all three of the town's newspapers told me about it right on the front page, in the kind of civic-pride tone most mining-town papers use to prove that they really are, after all, a bunch of law-abiding Christian people.

On a sunny June morning filled with bird song and silver dew, I sat in a crowded restaurant located between a lumberyard and a saddlery. The place smelled of hot grease, tobacco smoke, and the sweaty clothes of the laborers.

Near midnight I'd pitched from my dry and dusty mount and taken a room down the street at the Excelsior Hotel. I didn't know exactly what to expect from Gillian yet.

According to the *Gazeteer*, Rock Ridge was a town of four thousand souls, five banks, twelve churches (I found it curious that the *Gazeteer* folks would list banks before houses of the Lord), two schools, ten manufacturing plants, and a police department of "eighteen able and trustworthy men, among the finest in all the West." (On a following page was a small story about how a prisoner had died of a "mysterious fall" in his jail cell, and how his widowed mother was planning to sue the town, which of course told me a hell of a lot more about the police force than all of the newspaper's glowing adjectives.)

I was just about to ask for another cup of coffee when the front door opened up and a man in a dark blue serge uniform with shiny gold buttons on the coat came in, the coat resembling a Union Army jacket that had been stripped of all insignia. He wore a Navy Colt strapped around his considerable belly and carried in his right hand a long club that had an impressive number of knicks and knocks on it, not to mention a few dark stains that were likely blood that soap hadn't been able to cleanse. The contrast of his natty white gloves only made the club look all the more brutal. He had a square and massive blond head and intelligent blue eyes that were curiously sorrowful. He was probably my age, on the lee side of thirty.

He made a circuit, the policeman, like a mayor up for re-election, ultimately offering a nod, a handshake, a smile or a soft greeting word to virtually everybody in the place. And they grinned instantly and maybe a little too heartily, like kids trying hard not to displease a mean parent. They were afraid of him, and some of them even despised him, and the more they grinned and the more they laughed at his little jokes, the more I sensed their fear.

When he was done, he walked over to a plump serving woman who had long been holding a lone cup of coffee for him. He thanked her, looked around, and then settled his eyes on me.

He came over, pulled out a chair, sat down and put forth a hand that looked big and strong enough to choke a full-grown bear.

"You'd be Mr. Chase?"

I nodded.

17

"Got your name at the hotel desk. Always like to know who's staying over in our little town."

I said nothing, just watched him. Hick law, I figured, trying to intimidate me into pushing on. He wouldn't know anything about my time in prison, but he wouldn't want me around town, either, not unless I had some reason for being here.

"Name's Ev Hollister. I'm the chief of police."

"Nice to meet you."

"This is a friendly place."

"Seems to be."

"And we're always happy to welcome strangers here."

"I appreciate that."

"Long as we know their business." When he finished with this line, he shot me one of his empty white smiles.

"May be looking for a place to settle."

"You have any special trade?"

Yeah, I wanted to say, bank robbing. Which bank would you suggest I hit first? "Nothing special. Little of this, little of that."

"Little of this, little of that, huh?"

"Uh-huh." I gave him one of my own empty white smiles. "All strictly legal of course."

"Glad you said that."

"Oh?"

He took some of his coffee and wiped his mouth with the back of his hand. He was proud of those hands the way a man is proud of a certain gun. They were outsize, powerful hands. "Cholera came through here three months ago."

"Bad stuff."

"Struck the Flannery family especially hard."

"They kin of yours?"

18

"No, but they gave this town two of the best officers I ever had. Brothers. About your age and build. Damned good men." He looked at me straight and hard. "You ever thought of being a police officer?"

I could imagine the men back in territorial prison listening in on this conversation. They'd be howling.

"Guess not, Chief."

"Well, if you stay around here, you should consider it. The work is steady and the pay ain't bad, forty-eight dollars a month. And folks have a lot of respect for a police officer."

My mind drifted back to the mother of the youngster who'd died in a "mysterious fall" in his jail cell. I wondered how much respect she had for police officers.

"Well, I sure do appreciate the interest, Chief. How about I think it over for a couple days?"

"Lot of men would jump at the chance to be on my police force." There was just a hint of anger in his tone. He wasn't used to getting turned down.

I put forth my hand.

He stood up and made a big pretense of not seeing my hand sticking out there.

"You think it over," he said, and left.

The smile was back on him as soon as he reached the front of the place, where he flirted with a couple of ladies at a table and told a bawdy joke to an old man with a hearing horn. I knew it was bawdy by the way the old guy laughed, that burst of harsh pleasure.

Through the window, I watched Chief Hollister make his way down the street. The water wagon was out already, soaking down the dust as much as possible. A telephone pole was being planted on a corner half a block away. Ragged summertime kids stood watching, fascinated. Later they'd spin tales of how different a place Rock Ridge would be with telephones.

Up in the hills you could see the mines, watch the smoke rise and hear the hard rattling noise of the hoists and pumps and mills. In prison an ex-miner had told me what it was like to be 2,300 feet down when the temperature hit 120 and they had to lower ice down the shaft because that low your tools got so hot you sometimes couldn't hold them. And sometimes you got so dehydrated and sick down there that you started puking up blood—all so two or three already rich men in New York could get even richer.

And who would keep all those miners in line if they ever once started any kind of real protest?

None other than the dead-eyed man I'd just met, Rock Ridge's esteemed police chief, Ev Hollister. Over in Leadville they'd recently given a police chief and two of his officers $500 each for killing three miners who were trying to lead a strike. Law was the same in all mining towns.

I paid my money, went down to the livery and got my horse, and rode out to see Gillian.

4

It was a hardscrabble ranch house with a few hard-scrabble outbuildings on the edge of some jack pines in the foothills of the blue, aloof mountains. It was not quite half a mile out of town.

In the front yard a very pretty little girl of eight or so spoke with great intimacy to a dun pony no taller than she was. The little girl wore a blue gingham dress that set off her shining blond pigtails just fine. When she looked me full in the face, I saw the puzzlement in her eyes, the same puzzlement as in mine. She favored her mother, and that tumbled me into sorrow. I guess I hadn't any right to expect that Gillian would go without a man all these years. As for the little girl staring at me—I was long conditioned to people studying my scars, repelled and snake-charmed at the same time, but then I remembered my new blond beard that covered the scars. They couldn't be seen now except in the strongest sunlight. Yet the little girl still stared at me.

"I don't think I've ever seen eyes that blue," I said. She smiled.

"Are you enjoying the summer?"

She nodded. "I'm Annie. I bet I know who you are. You're Chase. My mom talks about you all the time."

It was a day of orange butterflies and white fluffy

dandelions and quick silken birds the color of blooded sunsets. And now fancy little conversations.

"I was going to write you a letter once," Annie said.

"You were?"

"Uh-huh, but Mom said I better not because of your major."

She smiled, sweet and shy and pure little girl there in the bright prairie morning.

"She said you were in the cavalry and that you had a real mean major named Thomkins who didn't want you to get letters."

I handled it best I could. "He was pretty mean all right."

"My mom's inside."

"You think it'd be all right if I went and saw her?"

"She's baking bread. She'll give you some if you ask."

I grinned. "Then I'll make sure to ask."

She put her tiny hand up in mine and led me up the earthen path to the slab front door of the ranch house. As we walked, I saw to the west a hillock where a well had been dug, probably an artesian that had failed because the water would not rise. Easier to walk to the distant creek and lug it back in buckets. Or make one of those homemade windmills you could now buy kits for.

I could smell bread baking. It reminded me of my own ma and our own kitchen, back before all the troubles came to us Chase boys, and for a moment I was Annie's age again, all big eyes and empty rumbling belly.

Annie pushed open the door and took me into the cool shadows of the house. The layout seemed to be big front room with a hallway leading to big kitchen in back. Between were two bedrooms set one on each side of the hallway. There wasn't much furniture, a tumble-down couch and chairs, a painting of an aggrieved Jesus, and a splendid vase lamp with an ornately painted globe. The flooring was hardwood shined slick and bright and covered occasionally with shaggy blue throw rugs.

In the kitchen, I found Gillian just taking a loaf of bread from the oven and setting it on the windowsill to cool. To clear room, she had to *shush* a cardinal away, and looked guilty doing it.

When she saw me there, led in by her little daughter, her face went blank and she paused, as if considering what to feel. I'd once promised Gillian I'd marry her, and never had; and when I was sent off to prison, she in turn promised she'd wait. But the birth of Annie had put the lie to that. I guess neither one of us knew what to feel, standing here and facing each other across a canyon of eight hard and lonely years.

She was still pretty—not beautiful, not cute, pretty—with a long fragile neck and fine shining golden hair, Annie's hair, and a frank blue gaze that was never quite without a hint of grief. She'd had one of those childhoods that not even a long life could outlive. She wore gingham, which she always had, and a white frilly apron, and even from here I could see how years of work had made her quick, slender hands raw. She was neither old nor young now, but that graceful in-between when a girl becomes full woman. She looked good as hell to me, and I felt tongue-lost as a boy, having no idea what to say.

"This is my mom," Annie said.

I laughed. "I'm glad you told me that, honey."

"He wants some bread."

"Oh, he does, does he?" Gillian said.

"And jam," Annie said definitively.

23

"Doesn't he know how to speak for himself?" Gillian said.

"He's so hungry, he can't talk."

I wondered, what had happened to that shy little girl who'd greeted me on the walk?

Gillian gaped at me a moment longer and said, "That sure is some beard you got there, Chase."

A few minutes later Gillian shooed Annie outside and set about fixing me up with that warm fresh bread and strawberry jam her daughter wanted me to have.

As she sliced the bread and poured us both coffee, she asked me how my first night here had gone, and I told her, with a laugh, all about how the chief of police had tried to recruit me.

"Maybe you should do it," she said.

"Huh?"

She set down my bread and coffee, slid the jam pot over to my side of the table, and then sat down across from me. "Maybe you should do it."

"Be a policeman?"

"There are worse ways to make a living."

"Seems you're forgetting where I've been the last few years."

"Hollister doesn't know where you've been. And he wouldn't have any reason to check unless you did something wrong."

We didn't speak for a time. She sat there and watched me eat. I tried not to smack my lips. I'd shared a cell with a man who snorted when he ate. I knew how aggravating noisy eaters could be.

When only my coffee was left, I looked up at her. "I'd appreciate it if you'd tell me about Schroeder."

"I was hoping you'd forget about Schroeder. Anyway, he calls himself Reeves now."

"What does he do?"

"Runs a bank. Has a partner who's very old, and lives in a big mansion by himself."

"The bank been robbed since 'Reeves' bought in?"

"No, but I imagine it's just a matter of time." She watched me the way Annie had when I'd first come into the yard. "Why don't you forget about him, Chase? That part of your life is gone now."

"He killed my brothers."

"They'd want you to go on with your life, Chase." She'd known both my brothers. While to the town they'd been bank robbers, to her they were never more than rambunctious boys who'd eventually settle down. "I knew them, Chase, and what they wanted for you. They didn't want you to be the way they were."

And then she was crying.

We were sitting in the kitchen with the scent of bread sweet on the air and a jay on the window ledge and the breeze soft and warm on the underside of the curtains.

And I didn't know what to do.

I just went over to her and knelt down beside her and took her tiny hand and held it gently as I could. I kept saying over and over, "Oh, Gillian, come on now; oh, Gillian, please," and things like that, but neither words nor touches helped, she just sat there and cried without sound, her frail body shaking with her grief.

And then Annie was in the doorway saying, "Did Chase hurt you, Mommy?"

Gillian got herself together quickly, brought apron to nose and eyes to daub tears, and cleared her throat sternly to speak. "No, hon, he didn't hurt me."

"I wouldn't like him if he hurt you, Mommy."

"It's fine, honey, really. You go on back outside now."

Annie looked at me for a time, confused and ready

25

to hate me if Gillian said to, and then turned and slowly left the doorway.

We sat in silence again until she said, "I don't want you to come out here anymore."

"Oh, God, Gillian. You don't know how long I've waited to—"

"I was hoping prison would change you. Force you to grow up and forget about Reeves." She sounded as if she were about to start crying again. "But it hasn't. I was just fooling myself all those years while I waited."

I wanted to point out that she'd been doing more than "waiting," what with having a daughter during that time.

But the words died in my throat, and I felt guilty for making Gillian carry on this way.

She put her head down on the table and started crying again, her slender shoulders shaking miserably. I leaned over and kissed her on the back of the head and slipped out through the gathering blue shadows of the afternoon.

As I walked over to my horse, Annie looked up from combing her pony and said, "Is my mommy still sad?"

I swung up in the saddle and said, "Right now she is. But if you go in and see her, she won't be."

She nodded solemnly, put down the brush she was using and set off walking to the ranch house.

5

"You got a name, son?"

"Chase."

"You got a first name?"

"Sorry. Guess people usually call me plain 'Chase.' First name's Robert."

"Well, son, I wish I could help you, but I can't. See that Indian out there on the loading dock?"

"Yessir."

"That sonofabitch does the work of three white men and he don't complain half as much as they do."

"Good worker, huh?"

"Good? Hell, great. That's why I don't need nobody right now. But I tell ya. If you're around town in three, four weeks, you try me again, 'cause you never can tell."

"That's right. You never can tell."

"Good luck, son, you shouldn't have no problem, big strong young man like you."

"Yessir. And thank you, sir."

That's how it went all afternoon. I went up and down the alleys, knocking on the back doors of every business I could find, and it was always the same story. Just hired me somebody last week; or business been a little slow lately; or why don't ya try down the street, son?

Near dusk, when I was walking into the lumberyard, I saw Chief Hollister and he gave me a smirk as if he knew that I wasn't getting anywhere and that I'd been damned foolish to turn down his offer.

As I had been.

6

That night, I sat in a chair next to Annie's bed reading aloud a book called *Standard Fairy Tales*. Nearby a kerosene lantern flickered light through the cottage.

"How tall was Jack's beanstalk?"

"Didn't you already ask me that?"

She giggled. "Uh-huh."

"It was eighty feet all."

"Last time you said it was sixty feet tall."

"I lied."

She giggled again. "You don't lie. My mom says you're a good man."

I looked up from my book to Gillian in the rocker in the corner. She was knitting. The rocker squeaked pleasantly back and forth, back and forth, as a slow summer rain pattered on the full-grown leaves of the elm trees on either side of the house.

"You said I was a good man?" I asked Gillian.

She smiled her easy smile. "I believe I said something like that, yes."

"Well, I just want you to know that I'm mighty grateful. It's nice to have somebody thinking nice thoughts about me."

"Did you really like my roast beef tonight?"

"I liked it very much."

"You didn't think it was tough?"

"I thought it was tender."

"You really mean that?"

"I really mean that."

Truth was, the meat had been tough as hell. Cooking had never been one of Gillian's strengths. Great baker—breads and rolls and pies—but terrible, terrible cook.

"I like to close my eyes and hear you read, Chase. I like it as much as Annie does."

"I'll read some more."

"I remember when you wrote and told me—when you were away, I mean—how that man taught you to read."

"When you were in the Army?" Annie said.

"Yes." I looked over at Gillian again. "When I was in the Army."

"Tell me about the Army. You promised."

"When we have a little more time, I'll tell you."

"Don't we have time now?"

"Nope."

"How come?"

"Because we've got to find out what the giant's going to do to Jack."

"Go on, Chase," Gillian said. "Annie and I'll close our eyes and you read."

So they closed their eyes and I read.

Later on that night, after Annie fell asleep, Gillian and I went down to the willow by the creek that ran in the back of her yard, and made love standing up, the way we used to sometimes in the old days.

When her dress was down and my pants were up, we walked along the creek listening to the frogs and the crickets and the owls. The rain had stopped and everything smelled minty and fresh in the midnight moon.

"You never did answer that one letter of mine, Chase."

"Which letter was that?"

"The one where I asked you if you'd ever say you loved me."

"I guess I figured you knew."

We walked a little more in silence. Stars filled the sky and everything smelled cool and fresh after the rain.

"Annie sure likes you."

"I sure like her."

"Says she hopes she sees you some more."

"Hope I see her some more."

We came to the small leg of river that ran below a railroad bridge. The water was silver in the moonlight.

I skipped rocks across the surface and she laughed and said it was good to see me acting so young; she'd been afraid that prison would make of me what prison had earlier made of an uncle of hers, a scared old man in a thirty-year-old's body.

About halfway back to the cabin I said, "Who's Annie's father, Gillian?"

"I was wondering when you'd ask me that."

"She's mine, isn't she?"

"Yes," Gillian said, "yes, she is."

7

Just in case you think that a policeman's life is filled with the kind of derring-do you read about in yellowbacks or eastern newspapers, consider the fact that I spent my first two days walking all over town handing out circulars that came from Chief Hollister. They read:

Cleanup notice is hereby given to property owners that all rubbish and disease breeding matter must be removed from their premises at once, or the work will be done by my officers at the owners' expense. The town board, sitting as a board of health, has ordered all pigsty and other nuisances to be abated. This order will be rigidly enforced.

(Signed) Chief of Police, Ev. Hollister

As you might expect, humans being humans, very little in the town was cleaned up by the owners, so most of us men, fine and shiny in our blue serge uniform coats with the bright brass buttons and the snug white gloves—most of us had to do the cleaning up. The men called it the "pig shit detail," and you got on it by drawing the smallest straw. I got on it twice in three weeks, which meant that Gillian had to do some extra hard cleaning of my uniform. But I don't mean to sound as if I was unhappy. I wasn't. My second weekend as an officer, Gillian and I got married, and my third weekend we sat Annie down and told her that I was her father and that we'd all be living together now forever. Annie cried and Gillian cried and I tried not to, but as I hugged them to me, I couldn't help myself. I cried at least a little bit, too. The hell of it was, I wasn't even sure why we were all crying. It was something the two females understood, not me.

In my first three weeks as an officer, I did not get into a gunfight, ward off an Indian attack, save a stagecoach from plunging into a ravine, rush an infant from a burning building, or even help an old lady across a busy street.

What I did do was spend from five in the afternoon till midnight six nights a week walking around the town and making sure that everything was locked up tight. Because what you had in a town like this, a mining town where bitter men drank a lot, was robberies. So my job was to walk a six-block area every night and rattle the doors on most of the businesses. I had been given the right to shoot on sight any burglar who offered me any resistance at all. I had also been given the key to most businesses so that in case I had to get inside, suspecting that a burglar might have hidden in there during business hours, I didn't have to bother Hollister or any of the merchants who were all home, presumably sleeping. At first, having the keys made me nervous— I'd never been one for much responsibility—but then as Gillian said over Sunday dinner, "You should be proud the merchants have that kind of trust in you, Chase."

Somewhere during those first few weeks, I gave up any notion of getting back at Reeves. I had convinced myself that Gillian was right, my brothers would have wanted me to pick up my life after prison and do something decent with it. Every once in a while I'd glimpse

Reeves swaggering down the street but I'd just turn my head and look the other way. I had a wife and daughter now and they were all that mattered.

Summer became Indian summer and Indian summer became autumn. By now most people in town knew me and seemed to like me. I enjoyed the feeling.

"That uniform looks good on you."

"Thank you."

"I'm glad I spotted you in the restaurant that day." It was just afternoon, and you could smell the whiskey on him but you couldn't exactly say he was drunk as yet.

I nodded. "Me, too, Chief."

I'd been going to the back for a drink of water, passing Hollister's office on the way. He'd called me in and started talking, sitting behind his desk with his feet up and his hands folded on his stomach.

He smiled. "Merchants're always asking me how I think you're doing."

"The keys?"

He nodded. "Yup. They want to make sure you're the kind of man they can trust. They like you and they want to keep it that way."

"So do I."

"We had a fellow here—three, four years ago, I guess—good fellow, too, least he was when he started, but by the end he was breaking into the stores himself and then reporting all these burglaries."

"He might have been good but he doesn't sound too smart."

Hollister started to say something but then peeked out his window and saw a fancy black surrey pull up outside the two-story red-brick police station. The surrey belonged to his wife. She was always out and about in

34

it. She had the kind of red-haired society-lady good looks that went just fine with a surrey like this one, and so naturally people resented her and whispered tales of her supposed infidelity. The police officers especially liked to tell such tales. It gave them a way to get back at Hollister, who always made it clear that he was at least one cut above us. He had been brought here by the merchants, and it was with the merchants he was friends. I'd even seen him eat lunch up to Casey's Restaurant with Reeves.

A minute later his eyes strayed from me and fixed on something over my shoulder. He smiled in a way that made him look ten years younger.

"Come on in and meet officer Chase," Hollister said in a smooth social voice.

I turned and saw her. She was a beauty all right, cat-green eyes to complement the silken red hair, nose and mouth and neck classical as a piece of sculpture. As she came into the room, she brought a scent of sweet cachet with her. In her crisp white blouse and full, dark green skirt, her hair caught up with a comb at the back of her head, she looked like a very beautiful schoolmarm.

"H-How are you d-doing?" she said to her husband.

That was the dirtiest part of the joke about Mrs. Hollister. Here you had all this beauty and grace and poise—she'd been schooled back East—and yet it was all marred by her very bad stutter, something she was clearly ashamed of. A lot of beautiful women like to flirt. They are saucy of eye and brazen of gait. But not Claire Hollister. She always walked with her eyes downcast, moving quickly, as if she wished she were invisible.

"Just a minute, hon," Hollister said, taking her hand

and stroking it gently. "I'll finish with Chase here and you can tell me about your day."

Hollister was a hard man and a dangerous man and a proud man, yet right now, speaking so softly to his wife, I heard real tenderness in him and I was almost shocked by it. He had a locked room upstairs where he took prisoners at night after he'd been drinking awhile. There was no tenderness in him then. None at all.

"I just wanted to say you're doing a good job, Chase, and that I'm glad you got married. A man needs some responsibility. Otherwise he's not much better than a hobo."

It was like an awards ceremony, all the nice words, only there wasn't any plaque.

"Thanks," I said.

I turned toward the door. Claire Hollister nervously got out of my way. She was a skittish woman, which made no sense with that beautiful sad face of hers.

"N-Nice to m-meet y-you," she said, and dropped her eyes, ashamed of herself.

"Nice to meet you," I said, and left.

8

With all the walking I did, I was pretty tired when I got home every night around one o'clock, the honky-tonk piano music still in my ears, the beery scent of the taverns I patrolled still on me. I'd eat the light meal Gillian had set out for me and then I'd go into Annie's room and kneel down by her bed and just look at her little face made silver by the moonlight, the stray damp wisp of blond hair making her look even younger than she was, and then I'd close my eyes and say the best prayer I knew how, a prayer that Annie and Gillian would always be safe in the invisible arms of the Lord, and a prayer that Hollister would never find out about my prison record and that I'd go on to be a good policeman who eventually got promoted. And then I'd lean over and kiss Annie on the forehead, her kid skin warm to my lips, and then I'd go into our bedroom and strip down to my underwear and climb in next to Gillian and hold her gently and think of how long she'd waited for me and how true she'd been and how her faith had given me this new life of mine, and all I could pray for then was that I would never give in to my worst self and go after Reeves.

The first time I ever saw Lundgren and Mars they were stepping off the train just about suppertime of an early November evening. Kids and dogs ran down the dark streets toward mothers calling them in for the night.

I don't suppose anybody else would have made anything special of them. They were just two middle-aged men in dark business suits, each carrying a carpetbag, each wearing a bowler, one tall and thin, the other short and heavyset. They stood on the depot platform looking around at the town. They tried very hard to give the impression that they were important men.

I was making my early rounds. After some months as a policeman, I'd already developed flat feet, bunions, and a suspicious eye for everybody and everything, and that included these two strangers.

I decided to follow them. They went down the boardwalk past the noise of player pianos and the smells of cigars and the laughter of whores, up past the livery where the Mex was rubbing down a horse that had just been brought in, and down past the gunsmith's.

I stayed half a block behind them, rattling doorknobs as I went, making sure the town was locked up tight. In the hills there was talk of a miner's strike. Socialism was just starting to get a grip on the miners. Hollister had told us to watch out for trouble.

This particular night, the two strangers ended their walk at the front door of the Whitney Hotel, the town's best hotel, and a place that always boasts of two presidents having slept in its hallowed beds.

When I'd given them sufficient time to find rooms for themselves, I walked up to the massive registration desk, turned the guest register around and stared at the names I'd been looking for.

"I don't remember inviting you to look at our registration book," said Hartley, the night man. Because he wears a cravat and attends all the musicales at the opera house, he seems to find himself superior to people like me.

But by now I didn't care what he'd said. I had their names and that was all I wanted.

"Next time I'd appreciate it if you'd ask me first," he said, petulant as ever.

"I'll be sure to do that," I said, being just sarcastic enough so he'd get the message but not so sarcastic that he could say anything.

Half an hour later I sat on the stoop of the police station, taking my dinner break.

In chill evening, the first stars showing, I heard the jingle of a bicycle bell and here came Gillian with Annie up on the handlebars, bringing me my dinner as they did every once in a while as sort of a special treat.

"It's getting nippy," Gillian said, handing me down a roast beef sandwich and an apple. "You can smell winter in the wind sometimes now."

Annie came over and sat down next to me. She couldn't get used to the idea yet that I was really her father.

"Did you shoot anybody tonight, Daddy?"

"Nope. But I wrestled a bear."

She giggled. "You did not."

"And when I got done with the bear, I wrestled an alligator."

More giggling. "Huh-uh."

"What're we going to do with this kid, anyway?" I said to Gillian. "She doesn't believe anything her old pappy tells her."

"Mrs. Dirks sent a note home with Annie today. She said Annie's one of her best students."

I gave Annie a hug and she gave me a wet kiss. The

temperature was dropping fast. Her little nose and cheeks were cold as creek stones.

"I'll have some stew hot when you get home."

"I'd appreciate that."

"I told Annie that maybe Sunday the three of us could go see the motor car over in Carleton County."

"That'd be fun."

"Goodie!" Annie said.

A minute later Annie was back up on the handlebars and Gillian was turning the bike in the direction of our cottage.

"Sleep tight," I said to Annie.

"I love you, Daddy."

"I love you, too, sweet potato."

And then they were gone, phantoms in the gray, starry gloom, the two most important people in my life.

Around ten I was finishing up with my second long patrol and just thinking of walking over to the bridge to roll myself a cigarette—I liked watching the river flow, and I couldn't even tell you why—when I looked down the street and saw two familiar shapes standing in the street in front of the Whitney Hotel. One tall, one short. Lundgren and Mars.

They stood for a time finishing off stogies, and then they flipped the butts into the street and walked on over to the livery. The Mex fixed them up with horses and saddles.

Five minutes later, seeming in no particular hurry, and seeming easy and confident on their mounts, the two of them rode out of town. I thought of going after them—they made me damned curious—but I knew it would take too long to get a horse saddled and follow them.

I stood there in the middle of the dark street, the

bawdy sounds of saloons behind me in the distance, the sounds of their horses loud but fading into the night.

Where would they be going at this time of night?

9

In the morning, after chores, I went into town earlier than usual. I couldn't stop thinking about Lundgren and Mars and what they might be doing in town.

The roan was fresh when I got him at the livery. A Mexican rubbing down a palomino gave me directions to the Reeves place.

An hour later, just as I rounded a copse of pines, I saw a massive Victorian house, a tower soaring up the center and seeming to touch the sky; a half-dozen spires; and three full floors. The front porch was vast and shadowy; the eaves elaborately carved. The grounds, enclosed within a black iron fence, looked relentlessly groomed. To the west was a large stable, to the east a vivid red barn.

It would take a whole lot of bank robbing to buy a place like this.

Just as I nudged the roan forward, I heard a rifle being cocked behind me.

"Howdy," a man's voice said.

He knew I'd heard his Winchester.

I tugged the roan to a halt.

"I said howdy, mister. Ain't you gonna howdy me back?"

"I'll howdy you all over the place if you'll put the rifle down."

"Just want to know your business out here."

"Far as I could tell, this is a public road."

"Yeah, but you ain't been on the road for ten minutes now. You been on Mr. Reeves' property."

A horsefly, having partaken of the splash the roan had just emptied on the road, buzzed near my face, loud in the sunny silence.

"You gonna say anything, mister?"

"I'm gonna say that I'm an old friend of Mr. Reeves'."

"No offense, mister, in case you are and all, but a lot of people say that to get inside here. They're usually looking for handouts."

"With me it's the truth, though."

"You got any way of proving that?"

"You just go tell Mr. Reeves that the man who helped him with his bank in Dunkirk is here."

"Didn't know Mr. Reeves ever lived in Dunkirk."

"You do now."

Now it was the guard's turn for quiet.

The cry of jays and the screech of hawks played against the lazy baying of the cows.

His shod horse took a few steps forward and he came around so he could take his first good look at me.

"You don't look like no businessman, son. Don't take that personal."

"Didn't say I was a businessman. All I said was that I'd given Mr. Reeves a little help."

He was fat and fifty but quick for his size, and his dark eyes gave you the feeling that he was capable of just about anything. He held a Winchester in gloved hands and spat tobacco in sickening streams, chawing not a habit I'd ever taken to as either participant or spectator. His sweated white Stetson looked too big for him, as if his head was shrinking in the heat.

43

"Name's Hanratty. What's yours?"

I told him. He looked as if he thought it was a fake.

"You ride ahead of me," he said.

"Past the gate?"

He nodded.

We went inside, along a cinder path, to the right of which an old black man was now raking leaves.

We ground-tied the horses in front of the long, shadowy porch. He took me up and inside the house. Two feet inside, a tiny, white-haired man in white shirt, paisley vest, and dark trousers appeared. He had a tanned simian face with bright brown intelligent eyes. He reminded me of a smart monkey. He carried a dust cloth in his right hand and a small bottle of sweet-smelling furniture polish in the other.

"Fenton, this man would like to see Mr. Reeves."

Fenton looked at me as if Hanratty had just told him some kind of joke.

"I see," he said.

"He looks unlikely as hell, I got to admit that." Hanratty laughed.

"Very unlikely," Fenton said. "And the nature of your business, sir?"

"Mr. Reeves and I once did a little business with a bank in Dunkirk."

"Dunkirk, sir?"

"Yes, he'll know what I mean."

"I see."

"So I wish you'd tell him I'm out here."

Fenton glanced at Hanratty again, then disappeared down the hall.

"I got to get back to my post," Hanratty said. "Good luck." He grinned and leaned to my ear. "Reeves ain't any nicer than he was when you knew him before, believe me."

I grinned back. "Nice to know some things never change."

I stood alone in the shadowy vestibule. Directly ahead of me a large, carpeted staircase rose steeply to a landing that glowed in sunlight. On the wall of the landing was a huge painting of Reeves in an Edwardian suit, trying hard to look like the illegitimate son of J. P. Morgan or some other robber baron. To my right was a wall with three doors on it, each leading to hushed rooms. The floor was parquet; almost everything else was dark wood, mostly mahogany. The effect was of being in a very fancy library.

Far down the hall, to the left of the staircase, a door opened. Footsteps—and Fenton—approached.

"Mr. Reeves will see you now."

He stayed several feet away. He didn't know what I had but he sure didn't want to catch it.

I went down the hall, the rowels of my spurs musical in the silence. I knocked on the door Fenton had just left, but nobody responded.

The door was open an inch or so. I pushed it open a bit more and peeked through. The room was a den with expensive leather furniture, a mahogany desk big enough to have a hoedown on, and enough leather-bound books to humble a scholar. There was a genuine Persian rug on the floor, and an imposing world globe sitting in its cradle on the wide ledge of a mullioned window.

I still didn't see anybody.

I took two steps inside, my feet finding the Persian rug. By the fourth step, hearing a human breath behind me, I'd figured it out, but by then it was too late. He did the same thing he'd done to me that night in my brother's room.

He came out from behind the door and brought something heavy down across the back of my skull.

My hat went flying and so did I.

"You sonofabitch. What the hell're you doing here?"

I was still on the floor, just now starting to pull myself up. I daubed the back of my head with careful fingers, finding a mean little lump and some blood.

Reeves sat behind his desk, a snifter of brandy near his hand. He was older and heavier, the hair gray-shot, and these days he looked like a successful politician in his dark suit and white shirt and black string tie.

"You're lucky I didn't kill you."

"I don't feel so lucky," I said, touching the back of my head again.

I got to my feet in sections and stood wobbling in front of his desk. Not until then did I realize that he'd slipped my .45 from its holster. I wondered how long I'd been out.

"As far as I'm concerned, our business is finished," he said. "You understand me?"

I reached down and picked up my dusty black hat and got it set just right on my head. I was taking everything slow and easy so as to not give him any warning.

I grabbed his snifter and splashed brandy in his face and then I dove across his desk and hit him twice before he finally pitched over backward in his fancy leather chair.

I could hear Fenton running down the hall—then banging on the closed door.

"Sir? Sir? Are you all right?"

He knew better than to let Fenton in. Otherwise I'd tell Fenton a few things he just might not know about his boss man.

"I'm fine. I just knocked the globe over is all."

"You're sure, sir?"

"Of course I'm sure. Now you get back to your dusting. We're having company tonight, remember?"

"Yes, sir." Fenton didn't believe him, but what could he say?

We got to our feet and took our respective places—him in back of the desk, ever in command, and me, dusty and busted, in front—ever the supplicant.

"You killed my brothers," I said.

He smiled. "Does that mean you're going to kill me?" But before I could answer, he said, "I've got something for you."

He opened a drawer, pulled out my .45 and slid it across the polished surface of his desk.

"Pick it up."

I just stared at it.

"Go ahead. Pick it up."

I picked it up.

"Now ease the hammer back and point the gun right at me."

He was a smug sonofabitch, sitting there in a couple hundred dollars' worth of clothes and a lifetime's worth of arrogance.

I had the gun but he was giving the orders.

"You're right, Chase—if that's what you're calling yourself these days—I did kill your brothers, and you know why? Because they let me. Because they were just like you, a couple of goddamned farm boys who just couldn't wait to rob banks because it was going to be so easy and so much fun." He shook his head. "Prison's filled with farm boys, as you no doubt found out." He leaned forward. He was het up now, a blaze-eyed minister delivering the truth to the unwashed. "It's a rough goddamned business, Chase, and I ought to know. I've survived in it twenty years now and it's made

47

me a rich man and I haven't spent one hour behind bars.''

"What happened to your partner after we stuck up his bank?''

The smile again. "Well, for once my partner figured something out for himself—figured out that I helped set up the robbery to make things go easy. He was about to turn me in, so I killed him.''

"You killed him?''

He shook his head, as if he were trying to explain a complicated formula to a chimp.

"I killed him, Chase. And that's the goddamned point which you never will understand. It's the nature of this business—of any business—to do what you need to when you need to.'' He sat back and made little church steeples of his well-tended fingers. "I'm able to do what I need to. How about you? Can you point that .45 of yours at me and pull the trigger?''

"You sonofabitch.''

"Never forget I gave you this chance.''

I cursed him again.

"Show me you're not a dumb goddamned farm boy like your brothers.''

I wanted to kill him, I really did, but I also knew that I wouldn't. Not under these circumstances.

"Go ahead, Chase. Otherwise you're wasting my time and your own.''

The gun felt good and right in my hand, and I could imagine the jerk of his body when the bullet struck his heart, and the red bloom of blood on the front of his lacy white shirt, and I could see my poor brother Don dying from the cuts and slashes the wolf had put on him, and I wanted so bad to pull that trigger, to empty the gun in his face.

"You sonofabitch.''

"You said that before, Chase. Several times." He stared at me. "I want you to learn something from this."

I didn't say anything.

"I want you to learn that you should go somewhere and buy yourself a little farm and find yourself a nice plump little farm girl and marry her and have yourself a bunch of kids and forget all about your dead brothers and forget all about me." He nodded to the .45 in my hand. "Because you had your chance. And you chose not to take it. And so what's the point of wasting your life hating me or trying to pay me back?"

Before, he'd reached to a right-hand drawer. Now he reached to a left-hand one.

He drew out a pack of greenbacks bank-wrapped with a paper strip around the middle.

He threw the pack on the desk.

"There's five thousand dollars there. That's about what your cut of the job would have been, as I recall. Probably a bit more, in fact. Take it, Chase; take it and get on that horse of yours and get the hell out of this county—get the hell out of this state, in fact—and go start the kind of life I told you to. All right?"

I stared at the greenbacks. I just kept thinking of my brother Glen's eyes when I'd cradled him in my arms as he was dying off the side of the stagecoach road, after Reeves had double-crossed us and taken the money and killed Glen because Glen had said something smart to him.

I could still hear the sounds Glen had made, those terrible sounds in his throat, dying sounds, of course, the way I'd once heard a calf strangle on its own umbilical cord one snowy night in the barn.

I stood up and pushed the money back to him and settled my gun in my holster.

"Oh, shit," he said. "You're still going to come after me, aren't you?"

"Two men came into town last night, name of Lundgren and Mars. And I'll bet I know why."

"Lundgren and Mars. Don't know anything about them."

But I could see the truth in his eyes. He knew damned well why they were here.

He tried to look relaxed, but mentioning the two men had infuriated him.

"You set foot on my property again, Chase, and I'll personally blow your fucking head off. Is that understood?"

I just stared at him a while, shook my head, and went back to the hallway.

When I got to the porch, Fenton was polishing some gold candelabras in the sunlight.

He said nothing, just watched me walk down the steps and start over to my horse.

It was then I heard the growl from somewhere on the other side of the house. I stopped, knowing right away the origin of the growl. The wolf that had killed my brother, the wolf of glowing coat and midnight-yellow eyes.

Fenton stopped his work and stared at me. "He's a killer, that one. The master would be just as well off shut of him, if you want my opinion. He's too dangerous."

I didn't say anything. I walked around the side of the house, and there, in a large cage made of galvanized wire, paced the wolf. In the sunlight his coat shone ivory; but his eyes, when his head swung up suddenly, were still the same odd yellow. An Indian was dumping raw meat through a small door in the cage. On the hot

50

wind you could smell the wolf's shit and the high hard stink of the grass he'd pissed in.

I walked closer and he started growling again, that low rumble I'd first heard when my brother Don was dying in his bed that long ago night.

The Indian, still on his haunches, looked over his shoulder. "He don't like you, man." He had graying hair worn long and a faded denim shirt and work pants. His feet were brown and bare.

"So I gather."

"He's a bad one, this wolf."

"Yeah," I said. "I know."

The Indian pointed to a hole in the ground where a small animal had burrowed up into the cage. "Raccoon. Should've seen what the wolf did to that little bastard." The Indian grinned with teeth brown as his skin.

I knelt down next to the Indian, gripping the wire with two fingers for support.

The wolf, who had been growling and going into a crouch, lunged at me suddenly, hurling himself against the cage and ripping his teeth across the two fingers I had inside the cage.

The pain was instant and blinding.

I fell back off my haunches, grabbing my bloody fingers and gritting my teeth and trying not to look like a nancy in front of the Indian who stood above me grinning again with his bad teeth and saying, "I told you, man, that wolf just plain don't like you."

I got to my feet, still hurting, but I pretended that the pain was waning. "Maybe I'll come back here some night and kill that sonofabitch."

The wolf was still glaring at me, still in a crouch, and still growling.

"He'd like to fight you, man. He really would."

I glared back at the wolf and left.

Hanratty was still at his post behind the jack pines, Winchester laid across his saddle. He waved, friendly as always in his way, but he didn't fool me at all. If he had to, he'd kill me fast and sure and never pay me another thought.

That afternoon, Hollister held one of his weekly meetings for the entire eighteen-man police force.

We stood in the back of his office, at full attention the way he'd ordered, while he gnawed on our asses the way a military man would.

He had plenty of complaints. One officer, and he said the man would know who he was, was found sleeping down by the mill. The officer would be docked ten dollars from his next check—this was damned near a fourth of the man's pay.

Then he held up his whistle and showed it around as if we'd never seen anything like it before. "Some of you seem to think it's embarrassing to use this—but I want you to use it anyway. Any time there's a crime, any time you're pursuing somebody, I want that whistle blown so that the citizens and your fellow officers know that you're carrying out your duties. When your fellow officers hear the whistle, they're supposed to lend you a hand. And when the citizens hear it, they're supposed to get out of your way." He held the whistle up for us to see again, put it to his lips and filled the slow golden afternoon air with an ear-shattering blow. Then he said, "If I catch anybody forgetting to use his whistle, I'll fine him five dollars." There was the usual grumbling.

The final matter was drunks. "Our friends Hayes and Croizer have been getting overeager again. Last Monday night they arrested two miners who were walking home drunk. How many times do we have to go over this, boys? We're not here to make the lives of working men any harder. Those poor bastards catch plenty of hell during the day—they don't need us to add to it. The rule is—unless a drunkard is causing some kind of trouble, he's to be left alone. If he's having trouble walking, then walk him home if you've got the time, or find a citizen to go get the drunkard's wife or son to take him home. But I sure as hell don't want any more people arrested just because they've got a snootful. Understood?"

We nodded.

"Good," Hollister said. "Now get to work."

We were just turning to leave when Hollister said, "Chase, I need to speak with you."

I turned around and faced him. He sat himself down and took a pipe from a drawer and put the pipe in his mouth and his feet on the desk.

"I kind of got my ass chewed on because of you, Chase."

I couldn't figure out what he was talking about but I got a sick feeling in my stomach. Hollister was known to fire men almost on a whim—especially if he'd been drinking, and he had that look now—and I could feel that old prison fear in my chest. But instead of getting locked in . . . this time I was going to get locked out— of a good job and wages.

"Because of me?" I said.

"That fop of a night clerk at the Whitney Hotel."

"Oh."

"You sound as if you know what I'm talking about."

I shrugged. "Hell, all I did was look at the guest register."

He smiled. "Without asking that sweet little man's permission."

I laughed. "So he complained?"

"Oh, did he complain. He had a letter waiting for me on my desk this morning. He was filled with civic outrage."

He sucked on his unlit pipe. "Western towns like ours hate police departments. Just about everything we do, the people consider infringing on their rights in some way."

He wasn't exaggerating. Two towns over, a group of outraged citizens, angered that the police chief had imposed a curfew following three drunken murders, took two young policemen hostage and threatened to kill them unless the police chief packed up and left town. The outraged mob had been led by the mayor and a minister. Eastern papers liked to talk about how the "Wild West" had been tamed now that a new century was about to turn. But that didn't mean that police forces—too often crooked and violent—had found acceptance, because in most places they sure hadn't . . . not yet, anyway.

"Why were you looking in the register anyway?"

For the first time I noticed that he was watching me carefully. He seemed suspicious of me.

"I saw two men get off a train. They didn't look right to me. I just wanted to see what names they registered under."

"Didn't look right to you?"

"Slickers, was how I had them pegged. Remember that confidence game that man named Rawlins was running on old folks a month ago? That's how they looked to me."

I didn't tell him about them taking late-night horses from the livery and riding out of town.

"You ask them their business?" Hollister said.

"No."

"That would've been better than bothering that sonofabitch at the Whitney. He's very popular with the 'landed gentry,' as they like to be called, and the 'landed gentry' likes to see us as a group of barbarians. This only gives them something else to bitch about.''

"I won't bother him anymore.''

"I'd appreciate that, Chase. You're doing a good job. I don't want to see you get in any political trouble with one of the mighty.''

"I appreciate the advice.''

He looked at my bandaged fingers. I'd put some iodine on them. They still smarted from the wolf bite.

"What's wrong with your fingers?''

I didn't want to tell him about Reeves. "I cut them when I was sawing some logs.''

He laughed. "You're about as handy as I am.''

When he laughed, he pushed a little breath up on the air. Pure bourbon.

I said good-bye and left his office. Before I even reached the doorway, I heard him sliding a drawer open.

I glanced back over my shoulder just as he was turning his chair to the wall so he could lift up his silver flask and tip it to his lips.

10

Before work next morning I took Annie up into the hills. She wanted to collect leaves.

I found some hazel thickets and showed her how to dig into the mice nests surrounding them. You could find near a quart of nuts that the mice had already shelled and put away for bitter winter. But we didn't take any, of course, because the food belonged to them.

Annie made a collection of the prettiest leaves she could find, taking care to pluck some extras for her mother, and then we stood on an old Indian bridge and watched clear creek water splash rocks and slap against a ragged dam some beavers had recently built. Annie counted eight frogs and six fish from up on the bridge.

We took the east trail back, watching sleek fast horses the color of saddle leather run up grassy slopes in the late morning sun.

When we got near the house, she stopped at the abandoned well. Four large ragged rocks formed a circle around the well, inside of which Gillian had placed a piece of metal to cover the hole.

Now, expertly, Annie bent down, lifted the piece of metal up, took one of her leaves and closed her eyes and said, "I have to be quiet now and keep my eyes closed."

"How come?"

"Because I'm making a wish."

"Oh."

"Mommy always says that's what you have to do for God to hear you."

"Be quiet and close your eyes?"

"Uh-huh. And drop something down the well that you really like."

And with that she let the pretty autumn leaf go from her hand. It floated gently down into the darkness.

Gillian had told me about the well, how it was pretty shallow, and how the folks who had the house before her got sick drinking from it.

"You glad you're my pop?" Annie said, opening her eyes. She'd heard a boy at school call his daddy his "pop" and had decided she liked it.

"I sure am."

"Well, I sure am, too." She smiled and put her hand in mine. "I always knew you were my pop."

"You did?"

"In my dreams I always had a pop. I couldn't exactly see him real good but he was always there. And then the day I saw you in front of our house—well, I knew you were my pop."

"Aw, honey," I said, feeling sad for all the years she hadn't had a pop, "honey, you don't have to worry about not having a pop anymore. I'll always be here."

"Always?" she said, squinting up at me in the sunshine.

"Always," I said, then reached down and swung her up in my arms and carried her home just that way, her blond hair flying and her laughter clear and pure. The only thing that spoiled it was the sore throat and aching muscles I had. I was apparently getting sick.

* * *

Around ten that night, I just happened to be standing half a block from the Whitney Hotel. And Lundgren and Mars just happened to be standing on the porch of that same hotel. They couldn't see me because I was in the shadows of an overhang.

Lundgren smoked a cigar. Mars just looked around. He seemed nervous. I wondered why.

Fifteen minutes after coming out onto the porch, Lundgren flipped his cigar away exactly as he'd done the night before, and then, also as he'd done the night before, led his shorter friend down the street to the livery where the Mex gave them two horses already rubbed down and rested and saddled.

Lundgren and Mars rode out of town, taking the same moonlit road as last night.

I finished my rounds of the block then cut west over by the furrier, where the smell of pelts was sour on the cold night. Moving this fast didn't make me feel any better. The damned head cold I'd been getting was still with me.

The alley behind the Whitney was busy with the usual drunks. Henry, a half-breed, had pissed his pants and was sleeping, mouth open and slack, propped up against a garbage can. A hobo with but one finger on his left hand was having some kind of nightmare, his whole body shaking and cries of "Mother! Mother!" caught in his throat. And there was Jesse—Jesse as in female, Jesse as in mother of three, Jesse as in town drunk. Most nights her kids (the father having been killed four years earlier in the mines) kept tight rein on her, but every once in a while she escaped and wandered the town like a graveyard ghost, and usually fell over unconscious in an alley.

I debated waking them and making them leave. But that would only mean that one or two of them would possibly remember me.

I made sure as I could that they were all sleeping, and then I climbed onto the fire escape that ran at an angle down the back of the Whitney.

I moved fast. I could always say that I was following a suspicious character up here. But I wouldn't want to use that excuse unless I had to.

Lundgren and Mars were staying on the fourth floor. I pulled the screen door open and went in. The hallway was empty. I started toward 406. In one of the rooms I passed, an old man was coughing so hard I thought he'd puke. The corridor smelled of whiskey and tobacco and sweat and kerosene from the lamps.

I was two doors from 406 when 409 opened up and a man came out. He was so drunk he looked like a comic in an opera-house skit. He wore a messy black suit and a bowler that looked ready to slide off his bald head. He was weaving so hard, he nearly fell over backward.

I pressed flat to the wall and stayed that way while the drunk managed to get his door closed and locked.

He didn't once glance to his left. If he had, he would have seen me for sure.

He tottered off, still a clown in an opera-house turn.

Shaking, neither my stomach nor my bowels in good condition, I went to 406 and got it open quickly. You learn a lot of useful things in prison.

The room was dark. Some kind of jasmine-scented hair grease was on the air. I felt my way across the room, touching the end of the bed, a bureau, and a closet door. By now I was able to see.

I started in the bureau, working quickly. I found nothing special, the usual socks and underwear and shirts without their collars or buttons.

I then moved to the closet. Nothing there, either.

I was just starting to pick up one of the two carpetbags sitting on a straight-backed chair when I heard footsteps in the corridor.

I paused, pulling my revolver.

In the street below there was a brief commotion as a few drunks made their way from one saloon to another. In the distance a surrey jingled and jangled its way out of town.

The footsteps in the hallway had stopped.

Where had the man gone? Was it Lundgren or Mars coming back?

My breathing was loud and nervous in the darkness. My uniform coat felt as if it weighed a hundred pounds. My whole chest was cold and greasy with sweat.

And then I heard him, whistling, or trying to—the drunk down the way, the one who'd barely been able to get his door locked. Easy enough to figure out what had happened. He had made his way down the stairs only to find that the people in the saloon wouldn't serve him. Too drunk. So he'd come back up here.

It took him several minutes to insert key into lock, to turn doorknob, to step across threshold, to walk across floor, to fall across bed, springs squeaking beneath his weight. Within thirty seconds he was snoring.

I went back to work.

I took the first carpetbag to the bed and dumped everything out. The contents included an unloaded .45, a few more shirts without celluloid collars, and a small framed picture of a large, handsome women I guessed was his wife. I took it over to the window and hiked back the curtain. A lone stripe of silver moonlight angled across the back of the picture: SHARON LUNDGREN, 1860–1889, BELOVED WIFE OF DUNCAN LUNDGREN. So he was a widower, Lundgren was. It made him human for me, and for some reason, I didn't want him to be human.

The second carpetbag didn't yield much more—not at first anyway. Mars was a collector of pills and salves and ointments. The bag had enough of these things to stock a small pharmacy. He seemed to be a worrier, Mars did.

I had almost given up on the bag when my fingers felt, way in the back, an edge of paper. I felt farther. An envelope. I pulled it out, winnowing it upward through tins of muscle ointment and small bottles of pills that rattled like an infant's toy.

I went back to the window and the moonlight.

I turned the envelope face up. In the left upper hand I saw the name and address of the letter writer. My old friend Schroeder, known hereabouts as Reeves.

The letter was brief, inviting Lundgren and Mars here to "increase their fortunes by assisting me in a most worthy endeavor."

I didn't have to wonder about what that "worthy endeavor" might be. Not when Reeves owned half a bank in town here.

I put the envelope back in the carpetbag and the carpetbag back on the chair.

I went to the door, eased it open, stuck my head out. The hallway was empty. In the hall I relocked the door, checked again to make sure that nobody was watching me, and then walked quickly to the screen door and the fire escape.

I knew now that I wasn't done with Reeves. Not at all, no matter how much I'd promised Gillian otherwise.

II

"He's going to do it again."

"He?"

"Schroeder. Reeves. Whatever name he goes by."

"Do what?"

"Hire two people to rob his bank and then double-cross them. Take the money and kill them."

"You sure?"

"Positive. Those two men I saw in town?"

"They're the ones?"

"They're the ones. I got into their hotel room to-night. They had a letter from Reeves."

She didn't say anything for a long time. We were in bed. The window was soft silver with moonlight. Annie muttered in her sleep. The air smelled of dinner stew and tobacco from my pipe. Somewhere an owl sang lonely into the deep sweet night.

"You promised to stay clear of it, Chase."

"I was just telling you who they are."

"You'll get in trouble. I know it."

"I didn't mean to make you mad."

She was silent. "I thought we had a nice life," she said after a time.

"We do."

"Then why do you want to spoil it?"

"I won't spoil it, Gillian. I promise."

"You promise," she said. "Men are always promising, and it doesn't mean anything."

I tried to kiss her but she wouldn't let me. She rolled over on her side, facing the wall.

"You know I love you, Gillian."

She was silent.

"Gillian?"

Silent.

I rolled over. Thought. Felt naked and alone. My sore throat was getting worse, too, and every once in a while, I'd shiver from chills.

I couldn't stop thinking about Gillian. How she knew what was going to happen now, with Reeves and all. How betrayed she must feel.

I tried to make it better for her.

"I'm not your father, Gillian," I said. "I'm not going to hurt you and I'm not going to run out on you the way he did. Do you understand that?"

But she didn't speak then, either.

After an hour or so I slept.

12

Next night, I made my rounds early. I had some business to do.

Lundgren and Mars put in their usual appearance at the usual time, strolling down the street to the livery, picking up their horses and riding out of town just as the moon rose directly over the river.

I rode a quarter mile behind them out the winding stage road.

They went just where I thought they would, straight to Reeves' fancy Victorian. But just before reaching the grounds, they angled eastward toward the foothills.

Half an hour's ride brought them to a cabin along a leg of the river. I ground-tied my horse a long ways back and slipped into the small woods to the west of the cabin. Everything smelled piney and was sticky to the touch.

When I got close enough to see through a window, I watched Lundgren and Mars talking with Reeves. He poured them bourbon. There was some quick rough laughter, as if a joke might have been told, and then quiet talk for twenty minutes I couldn't hear at all.

At one point I thought I heard a woman's voice, but I wasn't sure.

When they came out, Lundgren and Mars and Reeves, they were laughing again.

They stood making a few more jokes and dragging on their stogies and making their plans for the robbery.

"You don't forget about that side door," Reeves said.

"No, sir, I won't," Lundgren said.

Mars went over to his horse and hopped up. His small size made it look like a big effort.

"Talk to you boys soon," Reeves said, cheery as a state legislator on Flag Day.

Lundgren and Mars rode away, into dew-covered fields shimmering silver with moonlight.

Reeves stood there for a time watching them go, the chink of saddle and bridle, the heavy thud of horse hooves fading in the distance.

A woman joined him suddenly, as if from nowhere, slipping out of the door and into his arms. Silhouetted in the lantern light from inside, they stood there kissing for a very long time, until it was obvious that they now wanted to do a lot more than kiss. It took me a while to realize who she was.

A few minutes later Reeves slid his arm around her waist and escorted her back inside. They turned out the lights and walked back out and closed the door and got up in Reeves's black buggy.

Just before he whipped the horse, I heard her say, "K-Kinda ch-chilly out h-here t-tonight."

And then they were gone into the night.

There was a potbellied stove on the ground floor of the police station, and when I got back there, two men stood next to it, holding tin cups of steaming black coffee in wide peasant hands. Winter was on the air tonight.

Kozlovsky nodded upstairs. "Don't know where the hell you been, Chase, but the chief's been lookin' for you for the last hour and a half."

Benesh shook his head. "He's been drinkin' since late afternoon so I'd watch yourself, Chase. Plus he's got a prisoner up there in his little room. Some farmhand who got all liquored up because of some saloon whore. He made the mistake of making a dirty remark to the chief."

In their blue uniforms, the flickering light from the stove laying a coat of bronze across their faces, they might have been posing for a photograph in the *Police Gazette*.

"I'd better go see him," I said, coughing. I was feeling worse.

The two men glanced at each other as I left.

The "room" they'd referred to was on the second floor, way in the back beyond the cells, which were dark now, men resting or sleeping on their cots, like zoo animals down for the night. Every time I came up here, I thought of prison, and every time I thought of prison, I thought of all those old men I'd known who'd spent most of their adult lives in there. Then I always got scared. I didn't want to die in some human cage smelling of feces and slow pitiful death.

Halfway to the room, I heard the kid moaning behind the door ten yards away. I also heard the sharp popping noise of an open hand making contact with a face. The closer I got, the louder the moaning got.

I knocked.

"Yeah?"

"Chief, it's me. Chase."

A silence. Then footsteps. The door yanked open, the chief, sweating, wearing only his uniform trousers and shirt, his jacket on a coat hook, stood there with his hands on his hips, scowling at me. For all that the police officers and some of the citizens talked about Hollister's "torture room," it was a pretty unspectacular place, just bare walls and a straight-back chair in the middle of an empty room. Right now, no more than half-conscious, thick hairy wrists handcuffed behind him in the chair, sat a beefy farm kid. His nose was broken and two of his front teeth were gone. His face gleamed with sweat and dark blood, and his eyes showed terror and confusion.

"I've been looking for you," Hollister said.

"That's what I heard. I had to go home. My daughter Annie's been sick."

"Nobody could find you for over an hour, Chase. Don't give me any horseshit about your poor little daughter. Now you go downstairs and wait for me in my office."

He was drunk but you probably wouldn't have noticed it if you didn't know him. The voice was half a pitch higher and there was something wild and frightening in the blue eyes.

"You want me to put him in a cell?" I said, indicating the farm kid.

"I'll put him in a cell when I'm ready to put him in a cell."

"I wouldn't want to see you get in any trouble, Chief."

"I'll worry about that, Chase. You just go downstairs to my office and wait for me."

Just as the door closed, I glimpsed the kid in the straight-backed chair. His brown eyes looked right at me, pleading, pleading. I thought of the kid that day in the quarry, coming up and crying out for mercy. . . .

A moment later I heard a fist collide with a face. The kid screamed, and soon enough came another punch.

He was on the other side of a locked door now. There was nothing I could do.

I went back through the cells.

A man was lying awake on the cot, his eyes very white in the gloom. As I walked past his cell he said, "He gonna kill somebody someday, beatin' folks like that."

I just kept walking. Apparently the man was a drifter and hadn't heard that a prisoner had already died here in what the newspaper called a "mysterious fall."

Twenty minutes later Hollister walked into his office, sat down behind his desk, took a small round gold tin of salve from a drawer and proceeded to rub the salve onto the knuckles of his right hand. They looked pretty bad, swollen and bloody. He had his uniform jacket on now, and he once again appeared in control of himself.

"The sonofabitch tried to hit me," he said.

"That's a pretty neat trick when you're handcuffed."

He glared at me. "Are you accusing me of lying?"

I stared at my hands in my lap.

"Somebody in this town doesn't like you, Chase."

"Oh?" I raised my eyes and met his. He was sober now. Apparently, beating up people had a good effect on him.

He opened the center drawer of his desk, extracted a white business envelope and tossed it across his wide desk to me.

"This was waiting for me when I got to work this morning," he said.

"What is it?"

"You know how to read?"

I nodded.

"Then read it for yourself."

I opened the envelope, took out a folded sheet of white paper, and read what had been written on it in blue ink. The penmanship was disguised to look as if it was a child's.

The message was just one sentence long.

"It's a lie," I said.

"Is it?"

"Yes."

He took out his pipe, stuck it in his teeth and leaned back in his chair.

"It wouldn't be the first time, you know."

"The first time for what?" I said.

"The first time an ex-convict ended up as a police officer."

"I'm not an ex-convict."

"Whoever sent me that letter thinks you are."

"Somebody's just making trouble."

"How long were you in?"

"I wasn't in."

"Up to the territorial prison, were you? I hear it's not so bad there, at least not as bad as it used to be."

"I wouldn't know."

"The warden is a good friend of mine. I'm going to wire him and ask him a few things."

"Ask him anything you want."

He stared at me a long, silent moment. The clock on the west wall tocked. Out in front, around the potbellied stove, a man laughed.

"Your name really Chase?"

"Yes."

"Why were you in prison?"

"I wasn't in prison."

"Be a man, Chase. Tell me the truth."

"I robbed a bank."

"There. You said it. Now we can cut out the horseshit." He stared at me some more, tilted back in his chair. "You shoot anybody when you robbed this bank?"

"No."

69

"You ever shoot anybody?"

"No."

"So you're not a violent man?"

I shrugged. "Not so far, anyway."

He smiled around his pipe. "That's an honest way to put it. 'Not so far, anyway.' " He sat up in the chair. "I'm going to make some inquiries about you."

"Your friend the warden?"

"You can be a sarcastic sonofabitch, you know that?" He shook his head. "What I was going to say, Chase, is that except for your disappearance tonight, you've been a damned good officer. Everybody likes you and trusts you, especially the merchants, and that's very important to me. So believe it or not, I'm not going to fire you just because you raised some hell when you were younger. You've got a family now, and that changes a man. Changes him a lot." Hard to believe this was the same man who, half an hour ago, had been beating a handcuffed prisoner. "I'm going to write the warden, like I said, and if your story checks out—if you really didn't shoot anybody and if you were a good prisoner—then I'm going to forget all about that letter."

He put his hand out, palm up, and I laid the letter on it.

He checked the clock. "Hell, I'd better be going home. My wife was visiting her cousin tonight and she'll probably be getting home about now."

"You want me to keep working tonight?"

"Of course I do, Chase. If you've been honest with me tonight, you don't have anything to worry about."

"I appreciate this, Chief."

"Get back to work, Chase, and forget about anything except doing a good job."

I stood up, nodded good-bye, and left.

I had a cup of coffee out next to the stove and then I went back to work.

Ev Hollister was one complicated sonofabitch, and those are the men you always have to be extra careful of.

13

The young man with the white shirt and the celluloid collar and the fancy red arm garters peered at me from behind the bars of his teller's cage and said, "Three other police officers have their accounts here, too, Mr. Chase." He had a face like a mischievous altar boy. He wore rimless glasses to make himself look older.

I smiled. "Then I must be doing the right thing."

I hadn't ever wanted to step inside any bank that Reeves owned. But I wanted to see the place that Lundgren and Mars were going to rob, because by now I knew what I was going to do.

The layout was simple. For all its finery, the flocked wallpaper, the oak paneling, the elegant paintings, the massive black safe built into the wall, which resembled a huge and furious god—for all of that, the bank was really just one big room divided up by partitions into four different areas. The safe would be relatively easy to get to because, except for a wide mahogany desk, nothing stood in the way. Women in bustles and picture hats, and men in dark suits and high-top shoes, walked around, conducting whispery business. The air smelled of gardenia perfume and cigar smoke.

I looked over at the side door that Lundgren and Reeves had talked about the other night. It used to open onto the alley, I was told, before the bank had been remodeled. Now it was never opened for any reason, though I had the key to it on my ring.

"She's a beauty, isn't she?"

"Beg pardon?"

"The safe," the teller said. "Barely six months old. Straight from Boston. I doubt even nitro could open it." He smiled. "Saw you looking at her. Must make the police feel a lot safer."

"A lot."

"But that's Mr. Reeves for you."

"Oh?"

"Sure. Always buying the best and the newest and the most reliable."

Yes, I thought, and probably spending his partner's money to do it.

I started hacking then, so much so that it got embarrassing. This morning my throat had been so sore, I could barely swallow, and the chills now came on with a sudden violence.

"Well, here's my first deposit," I said when I'd finished hacking.

I handed the teller ten dollars. He found a smart little blue bankbook and took an imposing rubber stamp and opened the book and stamped something bold and black on the first page. He then turned the page over and wrote $10.00 in the credit column. Then he wrote the date in the proper place and gave me the book.

"It's nice to have you as a customer, Mr. Chase."

"Thank you. I'm sure I'll like doing business here."

"I shouldn't say this, being so partial and all, but I think we're the best bank in the whole territory."

"I'm sure you are."

With that I turned and started back to the front of the bank. Then the front door opened and there stood Reeves, sleek and slick as always, staring right at me.

He was obviously angry to find me here, but he couldn't say anything with all the customers wandering around.

He came in, closing the door on the bright but chill afternoon.

He walked right up to me and said, "I'm glad to see you're still wearing that uniform."

"The chief is a more understanding man than you give him credit for."

"Maybe I'll just have to write him another little note about you." He frowned. "Why the hell don't you just get out of this town, Chase? I'd even be willing to give you some money if you just took that wife and daughter of yours and left."

"How much?"

"Maybe ten thousand."

"Maybe?"

"Ten thousand for sure."

I grinned at him. "No, thanks, I kind of like it here. Especially when I get a chance to ruin your day like this every once in a while." I started out the door and then said, quietly, "Be sure to give Lundgren and Mars my best wishes."

He looked around to see if anybody was watching. They weren't. "You don't know what you're getting into, farm boy."

"See you around," I said, and left.

I stood on the boardwalk for a while, enjoying the pale, slanting sunlight, enjoying the town, really, the clatter of wagons and horse-drawn trolleys, the spectacle of pretty town women going about their shopping, the way folks greeted me as they passed.

They liked me, the town folks, and I enjoyed that feeling.

I was a happy man just then, and I walked down the street with my lips puckered into a whistle. I tried not to notice how bad my throat was hurting.

14

That night, feeling even sicker, I dragged myself home and went right to bed . . .

In the darkness.

"Chase?"

"Huh?"

"I wanted to wake you up. You were having the nightmare again. About the kid, I think."

"Oh."

"I'm sorry you had to see that, Chase."

"Yeah."

"It must have been terrible to see."

I was sweating, but it was cold sweat and I wanted to vomit. There was just the darkness. And Gillian next to me in her flannel nightgown.

"I said a prayer tonight, Chase."

"How come?"

"That you wouldn't go through with it." Silence. "I know it's on your mind."

"It could work out for us. A lot of money. Going somewhere and buying a farm."

We were silent for a long time.

"Annie saw me praying—I mean, I was down on my knees with my hands folded, just like I was in church— and she asked me what I was praying for, and I told her that I was praying for Pop, that Pop would always do the right thing."

The miners got paid on Fridays. On Friday morning the bank always got extra cash for payroll. Today was Friday. Lundgren and Mars would hit the bank today sometime.

"You hear me, Chase? About my praying?"

"You know I love you and Annie."

"It'll come to no good, Chase. Men like Reeves just go on and on. I hate to say this, but sometimes evil is more powerful than good. I don't understand why God would let that be, but He does."

Just the darkness, and Gillian next to me . . .

I wanted to be content and peaceful. I really did. But I just kept thinking of how easy it would be to take that money from Lundgren and Mars.

I started coughing hard, the way I'd been doing lately. She held me tight, as if she could make my illness go away. Sometimes she was so sweet I didn't know what to do with myself. Because I wasn't sweet at all.

"Chase, I want you to go see the doc tomorrow. I mean it. No more excuses."

I didn't say anything.

I lay back.

The sweat was cold on me. I was shivering.

"Chase. There's something that needs saying."

I didn't say anything.

"You listening, Chase?"

"Uh-huh."

"Chase, if you go through with this, I'll take Annie and leave. I swear."

I wanted to cry—just plain goddamn bawl—and I wasn't even sure why.

"I love you, Gillian."

But then I went and ruined it all by coughing so hard

I had to throw my legs over the side of the bed and just sit there hacking. Maybe Gillian was right. Maybe I needed to see the doc.

When I finally laid back down again, Gillian had rolled over to face the wall.

"Honey? Gillian?"

But she wasn't speaking anymore.

Both of us knew what was going to happen, and there wasn't much to be said now.

"You're going to do it, Chase," she said after a time. And I drew her to me and held her. And I could smell her warm tears as I kissed her cheek. "I know you are, Chase. I know you are."

15

I got up early, before the ice on the creek had melted off, put on street clothes and went into town. My bones ached but I tried not to notice. The sounds of roosters and waking dogs filled the chill air. The sky was a perfect blue and the fallen leaves were bright as copper pennies at the bottom of a clear stream. The fever had waned. I felt pretty good.

I went directly to the restaurant, ordered breakfast and took up my place by the window. I wanted to keep a careful eye on the street. I knew what was going to happen this morning.

Reeves arrived first, riding a big chestnut. In his black suit and white Stetson he was trying, as usual, to impress everybody, including himself.

He dismounted at the livery, left his horse off and then came back up the street to the bank. Ordinarily, like most of the merchants, he stopped in here for coffee before the business day started.

But today he took a key from his vest pocket and walked around to the alley on the west side of the bank, and then vanished inside.

I had more coffee and rolled a cigarette and listened reluctantly as a waitress told me about a terrible incident next county over where a two-year-old had crawled into a pig pen where two boars promptly ripped him apart and then ate him. She had a sure way of getting your day off to a happy start.

The stagecoach came in twenty minutes later, a dusty, creaking Concord with a bearded Jehu and two guards up top bearing Winchesters. If you hadn't already guessed that they were transporting money, the two men with the rifles certainly gave you a big hint.

The Concord stopped right in front of the bank.

The front door opened and Reeves came out. He looked dramatic with a fancy silver pistol in his right hand and his eyes scanning the tops of the buildings on the other side of the street.

The two guards jumped down. One hefted a long canvas bag and went inside. The Jehu had taken one of the Winchesters and was watching the street carefully. Reeves stood right where he was, looking vigilant for all the townspeople to see.

It took three minutes and it was very slick. They'd all obviously done this many times. At this point, anybody who tried to take the money sack would likely be outgunned.

Then the bank door closed, Reeves inside, and the two guards jumped back up top and the Jehu took the reins and snapped them against the backs of the animals, and the stagecoach pulled out.

The waitress with the dead baby story came back and gave me more coffee. She was young and chubby but with a certain insolent eroticism in the eyes, and a smile that made her seem more complicated than she probably was.

"You ever see so much money?" she said and nodded across the street. "They make that delivery every week, and every time I see it, I think of what I could do with just one of them bags of money."

"Buy yourself a house?"

"A house, hell. I'd take off for Chicago and New York and I'd have me the best time a farm girl ever had herself."

There was a certain anger in her tone that told me at least a little bit about how she'd been raised, and how she was treated in a town like this. If she had the money, she was going to tell a whole lot of people to kiss her ample ass. I understood her, but that didn't mean I liked her much. A hard woman is meaner any day than a hard man. Maybe I didn't like her because she was too much like me.

She drifted away to cheer up some other people. I kept on watching the street.

Around ten, Lundgren and Mars appeared on the steps of the Whitney Hotel. They wore their business suits and business hats and strode their important business strides as they made their way down the street amidst the clatter of wagons and the clop of horse hooves and the handful of lady shoppers on this beautiful autumn day.

They went straight to the livery.

A few minutes later they were back on this street, this time astride two big bays.

They rode straight out of town without speaking to each other or looking around.

I got up, paid my bill, went over to the livery stable, got myself a roan, and then walked it down the alleys to a place directly across from the bank.

Just after eleven, they came back into town riding two different horses. This time they were got up as dusty cowhands, not businessmen. They didn't look like their previous selves at all, which was just how they wanted it. Mars had what appeared to be a sawed-off shotgun in his scabbard.

I stood under the overhang as they rode down the

street. Lundgren stayed up on his mount. Mars dropped off, grabbing the sawed-off shotgun. I wondered about the shotgun. I couldn't believe Reeves wanted anybody killed. A robbery would get you a jury trial and a prison stretch. A killing would you get hanged some frosty midnight while a lynch mob stood beneath you, grinning.

They pulled blue bandannas up over their faces.

Mars started moving quickly now, up on the boardwalk. But instead of going in the front door the way I figured he would, he ducked into the alley and went through the side door. He had a key and he used it quick and smart. He opened the door and went inside.

It sure didn't make any sense, him having a key.

Lundgren leaned over and put his hand on the Winchester in his scabbard. He was ready for trouble when Mars came boiling out of the door.

I rode my horse to the edge of town, ten feet away from the small roundhouse where an engine was being worked on. You could smell the hot oil on the cool fall air.

Five minutes went by before I heard the shotgun blast which was followed by a long, nervous silence and then horses running hard down the dusty main street out of town.

Six-shooter fire followed the horses. I imagined it was Reeves, emptying his chambers, making it look good for the townspeople.

Lundgren and Mars appeared a few minutes later, riding hard. At the fork they headed west, which was where I expected them to head. I gave them a five-minute lead and went after them, keeping to grass so I wouldn't raise any dust.

They'd had it all planned and planned well.

They rode straight to the river, where business clothes

and fresh horses were waiting for them. In a couple of minutes they wouldn't look anything at all like the robbers. And they'd be riding very different horses.

They took care of the robbery horses first, leading them to the edge of the muddy rushing river where Mars took a Colt and shot both the animals in the head. The horses jerked only once, then collapsed to the ground without a sound. Lundgren and Mars pushed them into the river, where they made small splashes and then vanished. All I could think of was the hayseed kid the old con had drowned that day in the quarry. I cursed Mars. The sonofabitch could have just shooed the animals up into the foothills.

I also kept thinking of the shotgun blast back at the bank. Anybody who could kill an innocent animal the way they had would have no trouble killing a human.

They took the long sack of money, wrapped it in a red blanket, and cinched it across the back of Mars' mount.

They stripped down to their longjohns and then put on their business suits and climbed up on their business horses and took off riding again, though this time they went slow and leisurely, like easterners eager to gasp at the scenery. At the river they threw all their robbery clothes into the rushing, muddy water.

Fifteen minutes later they came to the crest of a hill and looked down on the cabin where they'd been meeting Reeves, and where Reeves had been meeting Ev Hollister's wife.

They rode straight down the dead brown autumn grass, coming into a patch of hard sunlight just as they reached the valley.

A few minutes later, Lundgren tied up the horses and Mars lugged the money sack into the big, fancy cabin.

I sat there for a while, rolling myself a cigarette and giving them a little time.

After a while I grabbed the rifle from my scabbard and started working my way down the hill.

16

I went down the hill at an angle to the cabin and then along a line of scrub pines to the right of the place. There were no side windows, so that helped make my appearance a complete surprise.

I crawled low under the front window then stood up when I was directly in front of the door.

I raised my boot and placed it right above the doorknob, where it would do the most good. If my kick didn't open the door the first time, I was likely going to get a chest full of lead before I had a second chance.

The door slammed backward.

I put two bullets straight into a Rochester lamp hanging over a large mahogany table that looked just right for both a good meal and a poker game.

The Rochester lamp exploded into several large noisy chunks.

I went inside.

Lundgren and Mars were standing by the bunk beds, the money fanned out on the lower bunk.

They were just now going for their guns, but it was too late.

I crushed Lundgren's gun hand with a bullet. His cry filled the room.

"Throw the gun down," I said to Mars.

Lundgren had already dropped his when the bullet went smashing into his flesh and bone.

"Who the hell are you?" Mars said.

"Who the hell do I look like?" I said. "I'm a police officer from town."

"I'm impressed."

"You want me to shoot your hand up the way I did his?"

"Asshole," he said.

But he dropped his gun.

"Fill the sack."

"What?"

"Fill the sack."

"That's our money," Mars said. He was one of those belligerent little men whose inferiority about their size makes them dangerous.

"Do it," Lundgren said.

He had sat himself down on a chair and was holding his hand out away from him and staring at it. He was big and blond and Swedish. Tears of pain made his pale blue eyes shine. He was sweating a lot already and gritting tobacco-stained teeth.

"You heard what your partner said," I said to Mars.

"Maybe I don't care what my partner said."

I pointed the rifle directly at his chest. "I don't give a damn about killing you. After what you did to those horses, I'd even enjoy it."

"Do it," Lundgren said again. "Give him the goddamned money."

He was almost pathetic, Lundgren was, so big and swaggering before, and only whimpering and whining now. You just never know anything about a man till he faces adversity.

"He isn't going to turn this money in," Mars said, staring at me.

"What?" Lundgren said.

"You heard me. He isn't going to turn this money in. This is for himself."

"Bullshit. He's a police officer."

"So what he's a police officer? Half the goddamned cops we know in Denver are crooked. Why shouldn't they have crooked cops in a burg like this?"

"Fill the sack," I said.

Mars glared at me now, a tough little man in a brown business suit and a comic black bowler. He looked out of place amidst the expensive appointments of a stone fireplace, a small library filled with leather-bound classics, and leather furniture good enough to go in the territorial governor's office. He didn't belong in such a world.

"Fill it," I said.

"I'm going to find you, you piece of shit, and when I find you, I'm going to cut your balls off and feed them to you, the way the A-rabs do, you understand me?"

In two steps I stood right in front of him. As I brought the rifle down, I thought of how he'd killed the horses, and so I put some extra power into it.

I got him just once, but I got him square in the mouth, and so the butt of my rifle took several teeth and cut his lip so deep a piece of it just hung there like a flap.

He didn't give me the satisfaction of letting me hear his pain. Unlike Lundgren, he was tough. He had tears in his eyes and he kept making tight fists of his hands, but beyond his initial cry, he wasn't going to give me anything.

"Now fill it," I said.

This time he filled it, all the while sucking on the blood bubbling in his mouth.

When he was finished, I said, "Tie it shut."

"You tie it shut."

I hit him again, this time with the butt of the rifle right against his ear.

The blow drove him to his knees and he fell over clutching his head. This time he couldn't stop himself from moaning.

"Get up and tie the sack shut and hand it to me, you piece of shit."

"You hurt him enough," Lundgren said.

"Not as bad as he hurt those horses."

Mars got to his feet slowly, in a daze, swearing and whimpering and showing me, for the first time, fear.

He tied the bag shut with cord and then raised it and dropped it at my feet.

I couldn't get the horses out of my mind. I hit him again, a good clean hit against his temple.

He went down quick and final, out for a long time. His head made a hollow sound when it crashed against the floor.

"You sonofabitch," Lundgren said. "He'll hunt you down, you wait and see."

He was still holding his hand. Blood had dripped on his nice black boots and all over the floor.

I hefted the bag, holding the rifle in my right hand.

"You'll want to know my name so you can tell Reeves," I said.

"How the hell do you know about Reeves?"

I didn't answer his question. "My name's Chase. He'll know who I am."

"You sonofabitch. You're fucking with the wrong people, you better believe that."

I backed up to the door.

"Remember the name," I said. "Chase."

"You don't worry. I won't forget it. And neither will Mars."

I went out the door and into the warming sunshine

of late morning. I could smell the smoky hills and hear a jay nearby.

I walked around the cabin to where they'd ground-tied their horses. I shooed one away and then climbed up on the other.

I went up the hill fast. When I got to my own horse, I jumped down, put the money sack across his back, and then shooed the other horse away. He went straight across the hill and disappeared behind some scrub pines.

I got up on the roan and rode away.

17

An hour later, I dismounted, eased the money sack down from the horse and then carried it, along with a good length of rope, over to the abandoned well near our house.

I knelt down, lifted up the metal cover and peered down inside. Sometimes you could go down a couple of hundred feet and still hit shale. But Gillian had said this one had been easy, the water right there, just waiting. I took out my spike and the hammer I'd grabbed from my saddlebag and drove the spike deep into the shale on the side of the well. Then I took a piece of rope and tied one end to the top of the money bag and the other end to the spike. And then I fed the money bag, an inch of rope at a time, down into the well, stopping just short of the waterline. Nobody would think to look here. I pulled the cover over the well again and stood up.

Overhead, an arcing falcon soared against the autumn sky, swooping down when its prey was clearly in sight. I stood and watched until it carried a long black wriggling silhouette of a snake up into the air.

I stood there and thought about it all, what I'd done and what lay ahead, and what Gillian would say and how brokenhearted she'd be unless I could convince her that I'd done the right thing; and then I got on my horse and rode into town.

18

Three hours after the robbery, people still stood in the street, staring at the bank and talking about everything that had happened.

On my way to the station, an old man carrying a hearing horn stopped me and said, "You catch those bastards, hang 'em right on the spot far as I'm concerned."

I nodded.

"That kid just died," he said, "a few minutes ago."

I rode another half block and saw Dr. Granville, a pleasant, chubby middle-aged man always dressed in a black three-piece suit to match his black bag. He was a real doctor, educated at a medical school back East, not just a prairie quack the way so many of them are.

He was crossing the dusty street, and when he saw me, he said, "Terrible business. I remember delivering that kid, the one that got killed. Hell, he wasn't twenty years old yet."

I went on down the street. I was stopped by half a dozen citizens who wanted to express their anger over what had happened to the clerk.

I took my horse to the station and tied him up in back and went inside.

I was just passing Ev Hollister's office when I heard a familiar voice.

"I'm doing what I have to, Hollister, nothing more and nothing less."

He spoke, as usual, with a small degree of anger and a great degree of pomposity.

He sounded riled and he sounded rattled, and I wanted to get a look at him this way, so I leaned in the door frame and watched him as he bent over the chief's desk.

"Something I can do for you?" Hollister said when he saw me.

"I just rode in from town and heard that the bank was robbed."

As I said this, Reeves turned around and faced me. His look of displeasure was deep and pure.

"Yeah, and one of the tellers was killed. Had a gun in his cash drawer. Just a kid, too. Briney."

Briney was the youngster who'd opened my account. The one with the rimless glasses and the altar boy smile.

"Specifically against my orders," Reeves said. "I specifically forbid my tellers to keep guns in their drawers. I didn't want anything like this to happen."

Reeves wasn't angry only at me. He was also angry at Lundgren and Mars. A robbery would get a town riled. But the murder of a young man would put them in the same mind as that old man I'd just seen on the street. They'd want a hanging.

Reeves scowled at me. "What I want to know is how the robber got the key to the side door of the bank."

That had troubled me, too.

Hollister shifted forward in the chair behind his desk and started cleaning his pipe bowl with a pocketknife.

"Reeves here thinks the robbers got the key from somebody who had access to the bank."

"One of the employees?" I said.

93

Hollister shook his head. "Huh-uh. Bank employees aren't given keys."

"Could one of the employees have stolen it?" I said.

"Reeves says no." Hollister spoke as if Reeves weren't here. "Says the only person with a key is himself."

"And one other man," Reeves said, his eyes fixed on my face. "You."

I looked at Hollister. His face was drawn and serious. "You know where the keys are, Chase?"

"In the drawer in the back room. Where I always leave them when I finish my shift at night."

"You never take them home?"

"Never. You said not to."

Hollister nodded somberly toward the back. "Why don't you go get that ring of keys and bring it up here?"

I looked at Reeves. He was still scowling. "All right," I said.

My bones were still aching and I was starting to cough some, but those problems were nothing compared to what I was beginning to suspect.

In the back room, where Hollister posts the bulletins and directives for the men, I got into the desk where all the junior officers sit when they have to write out reports.

Left side, second drawer down, I found the keys. Usually there were seventeen in all. Today there were sixteen. I counted them again, just to make sure that my nerves hadn't misled me. Sixteen. The bank key was missing.

I sat there for a long time and thought about it. It was pure Reeves and it was pure beautiful, the way he was about to tie me in with Lundgren and Mars.

I went back up front. I set the keys on Hollister's desk.

He looked down at them and said, "Well, Chase?"

"There's one missing."

"You know which one that is?"

"Yes, sir."

"The bank key?"

"Yes, sir," I said.

"I knew it," Reeves said. "I goddamn knew it."

"I didn't take that key, Chief."

Hollister nodded. "I believe you, Chase, but I'm afraid Reeves here doesn't."

I met Reeves' gaze now. There was a faint smile on his eyes and mouth. He was starting to enjoy himself. If only one person had the key to the bank other than himself, then who else could the guilty party be?

I stood there feeling like the farm boy I was. I'd never been gifted with a devious mind. Reeves had not only robbed his own bank, he had also managed to set me up in the process—set me up and implicate me in the robbery.

"A little later," Hollister said quietly, "you and I should talk, Chase."

I nodded.

"Why don't you go ahead and start your shift now?" Hollister said.

"Yes, Chase, you do that," Reeves said. "But you can skip the bank. Thanks to you, there isn't any money left in there."

It was a long afternoon. The sun was a bloody red ball for a time and then vanished behind the piney hills, leaving a frosty dusk. Dinner bells clanged in the shadows and you could hear the *pock-pock-pock* of small feet running down the dirt streets for home. The only warmth in the night were the voices of mothers calling in their young ones. If there was concern and a vague alarm in the voices—after all, you could never be quite sure that your child really was safe—there was also love, so much so that I wanted to be seven or eight again and heading in to the dinner table myself, for muttered Praise the Lords and some giggly talk with my giggly little sister and some of my mother's muffins and hot buttery sweet corn.

There were a lot of fights early that night. The miners, learning that they would have no money tomorrow, demanded credit and got it and drank up a lot of the money they would eventually get. In all, I broke up four fights. One man got a bloody eye with the neck of a bottle shoved in his face, and another man got two broken ribs when he was lifted up and thrown into the bar. The miners had to take their anger out on somebody, and who was more deserving than a friend? Like most drunkards, they saw no irony in this.

Just at seven Gillian and Annie brought my dinner, cooked beef and wheat bread. It was too cold for them to stay, so they started back right away—but not before Gillian said, "Annie, would you wait outside a minute?"

She studied both of us. Obviously, just as I did, Annie sensed something wrong. She looked hurt and scared, and I wanted to say something to her, but when Gillian was in this kind of mood, I knew better.

Annie went out the back door of the station, leaving Gillian and me next to the potbellied stove in the empty room.

"There was a robbery this morning, Chase," she said.

"So I heard."

"Reeves' bank."

"Right."

"He did it again, didn't he?"

"Did what?"

96

"Did what? God, Chase, don't play dumb. You know how mad that makes me."

"There was a robbery, yes, and it was Reeves' bank, yes, but other than that, I don't know what you're talking about."

She studied me just as Annie had. "Chase."

"Yeah?"

"I made up my mind about something."

"Oh?"

"If you take that bank robbery money, I'm going through with what I said. About leaving you. I'm going to pack Annie and I up and go and that's a promise. I don't want our daughter raised that way."

"He killed my two brothers."

"Don't give me that kind of whiskey talk, Chase. Your brothers are dead and I'm sorry about that, but no matter what you do, you can't bring them back. But you can give Annie a good life, and I'm going to see that you do or I'm taking her away."

"I love you, Gillian."

"This isn't the right time for that kind of talk, Chase, and you know it."

She walked to the door and turned around and looked at me. "If you break her heart, Chase, or let her down, I'm never going to forgive you."

She went right straight out without saying another word, or giving me a chance to speak my own piece.

The fights went on all night. A Mex took a knife to a miner who kept calling him a Mex, and two miners who should have known better got into a drunken game of Russian roulette. They both managed to miss their own heads, but they shot the hell out of the big display mirror behind the bar.

Just at eleven, when I was finishing my second sweep

of the businesses, making sure all the doors were locked, making sure that no drunken miners had sailed rocks through any of the windows, I was walking past an alley and that was when they got me.

They didn't make any noise and they surprised me completely.

Mars hit me on the side of the head with the butt of a .45, and Lundgren dragged me into the shadows of the alley.

"Where's our money?" Lundgren said.

I didn't answer. Wouldn't. Because no matter what he did to me, it wasn't going to be his money ever again.

Mars took the first three minutes. He worked my stomach and my ribs and my chest.

At one point I started throwing up, but that didn't slow him down any. He had a rhythm going, and why let a little vomit spoil everything?

By the time Mars finished, I was on my knees and trying to pitch forward.

Lundgren had better ideas.

He grabbed me by the hair and jerked me to my feet and then started using his right knee expertly on my groin.

He must have used it six, seven times before I couldn't scream anymore, before I let the darkness overwhelm me there in the dust that was moist with my own blood and sweat and piss . . .

Just the darkness . . .

19

Six years ago, two Maryknoll nuns on their way to California stopped through here. They stayed just long enough, I'm told, to set up an eight-bed hospital. It's nothing fancy, you understand, but there's a small surgery room in addition to the beds, and everything is white and very clean and smells of antiseptic.

Doc Granville got me into his examination room but then had to go out to get a man some pills. Apparently, people felt comfortable stopping by at any hour. While I was in the room alone, I looked through his medical encyclopedia. There was something I needed to look up.

When I was finished, I went back to the table and laid down and Doc Granville came in and got to work.

He daubed some iodine on the cut across my forehead. I winced. "Hell, son, that don't hurt at all."

"If you say so."

"Miners do this to you? I know they're raising hell because their paychecks are going to be late."

"I didn't get a real good look at them. But I think it was Mexes."

"You must be at least a little bit tough."

"Why's that?"

"That beating you took. And you're up and around."

I thought of mentioning what I'd just read. I decided

not to. Things were complicated enough. "I'm not up and around yet."

He laughed. "I don't hand out that many compliments, son. Just accept it with some grace and keep your mouth shut."

I smiled at him. For all his grumpiness, he was a funny bastard, and a pretty decent man at that.

The pain was considerable. He had me on the table with my head propped up. He'd fixed the cuts on my face and then carefully examined my ribs. They were sore. Not broken, he said, but probably bruised. I tried not to think about it.

He was about to say something else when knuckles rapped on the white door behind him.

"I told you I'd be out in five minutes, nurse. Now you just hold on to your britches."

"It's not the nurse."

And it wasn't.

"Your boss," Granville said in a soft voice.

I nodded.

"They're going to hurt like a bitch when you get up, those ribs of yours."

"I imagine."

"Nothing I can do for it except tape it up the way I did."

"I appreciate it."

He went to the door and opened it.

Hollister, in his blue serge, walked into the room with the kind of military precision and stiffness he always used when he was trying to hide the fact that he'd been drinking.

He nodded to Granville and came straight over to me. He scowled when he saw my face.

"What the hell happened?"

So I told him the Mex story, the same one I'd told

Granville. It was better the second time around, the way a tall tale usually is, but as I watched him, I could see he didn't believe a word of it.

"Mexes, huh?"

"Uh-huh."

"Two of them."

"Uh-huh."

"I'm told you didn't sound your whistle," he said.

"I didn't have time."

"Or use your weapon."

"I didn't have time for that, either."

"They just grabbed you . . ."

"Grabbed me as I was walking past an open alley."

"And dragged you . . ."

"Dragged me into the alley and—"

"Why did they drag you into the alley?"

"Because I saw them in the alley, fighting—one of them even had a knife—and I told them to stop, and they turned on me."

"Just like that?"

"Just like that."

"Before you could do anything?"

"Before I could do anything."

Granville was watching me, too. He was pretending to be sterilizing some of his silver instruments, but he was really watching Hollister try to break my story.

Hollister suddenly became aware of the doc. "You do me a favor, Doc?"

"Sure, Ev."

"Wait outside."

"If you want."

"I'd appreciate it."

"Sure."

Doc looked like a kid disappointed because he had

to stay home while all his friends went off and did something fun.

Doc went out and closed the door.

Hollister didn't talk at first. He went over and picked up a straight-backed chair and set it down next to the table I was lying on. Then he took out his pipe and filled it and took out a stick match and struck it on the bottom of his boot. The room smelled briefly of phosphorous from the match head and then of sweet pipe tobacco.

He still didn't say anything for a long time, but when he did speak, it sure was something I paid attention to.

"Only one way those two boys that stuck up the bank could've gotten that key."

I didn't say anything.

He said, "How much did they promise you, Chase?"

I still didn't say anything. I just lay there with my ribs hurting every other time I inhaled. I had never felt more alone.

"Reeves estimates that they got away with fifty thousand. If they didn't give you at least a third of it, you're not a very good businessman."

"I didn't have anything to do with the robbery, Chief. I honestly didn't."

"I took a chance on you, being an ex-convict and all."

"I know that and I appreciate it."

"And now here I am kicking myself in the ass for doing it."

"I'm sorry, Chief."

"Every single merchant in this town knows what happened, how you threw in with those robbers."

"I didn't, Chief. I really didn't."

I closed my eyes. There was nothing else to say.

"They didn't hesitate to kill that clerk at the bank this morning, and they sure won't hesitate to kill you."

He puffed on his pipe. "That beating they gave you was just a down payment, Chase."

He was trying to scare me. I thought of scaring him right back by telling him about that wife of his and Reeves.

He stood up and walked over to the table and faced me.

He jabbed a hard finger into my taped-up ribs.

I let out a cry.

"They worked you over pretty good. Maybe you should take a few days off."

"Is that an order?"

He sighed. "I can't prove you actually gave them that key, so I'm not going to fire you, even though every merchant in town wants me to."

"That's white of you."

He shook his head. "Chase, I thought you were smarter than all this."

"I didn't throw in with them, no matter what you say."

"Then where did they get the key?"

I stayed quiet. I didn't want to drag Reeves into this. That would only complicate things.

"You got any answer for that, Chase?"

"I don't know where they got the key."

"But not from you?"

"Not from me."

He took the last noisy drags of his pipe. "You've got a nice wife and a nice little girl. You don't want to spoil things for them."

"I sure don't."

"Then I'm going to ask you once more, and I want you to tell me the truth."

"You don't even have to ask. I didn't give them the key."

He walked over to the door. His boots walked heavy on the boards of the floor.

"You going to tell me why they came after you?"

"I told you. It was two Mexes."

"Right. Two Mexes."

"And they were drunk."

"Real drunk, I suppose."

"Right," I said. "Real drunk."

He looked sickened by me. "You're wasting your goddamned life, Chase. You've gotten yourself involved in something that's going to bring down your whole family. And you're going to wind up in prison again. Or worse."

He didn't even look at me anymore. He just walked through the doorway, slamming the door hard behind him.

I lay there, quiet, still hurting from where he'd jammed his finger into my rib.

20

Gillian put a match to the kerosene lamp and then held the light close to my face and looked over what they'd done to me.

I watched her closely in the flickering lamplight, older-looking tonight than usual, her eyes moving swiftly up and down my face, showing no emotion at all when she got to the black and blue places. She didn't touch me. I knew she was angry.

I'd been home ten minutes, sitting at the kitchen table, rolling a cigarette in the dark, trying to wake neither Gillian nor Annie, but then I'd dropped my cigarette, and when I went to get it, my rib hurt so bad I made a noise, and that had awakened Gillian.

Now she finished with her examination and set the lamp down in the middle of the table and went around and sat across the table from me.

She just kept biting her lip and frowning.

"Two Mexes," I said, keeping my voice low with Annie asleep in the other room.

"Don't say anything, Chase."

"I'm just trying to explain—"

"You're not trying to explain anything. You're lying, that's what you're doing."

"But Gillian, listen—"

"You got yourself involved in that robbery somehow,

105

and it all went wrong just the way I knew it would, and now Reeves is after you.''

She started crying. No warning at all.

I sat there in the lamp-flick dark with the woman I'd loved so long, knowing how much I'd let her down. To get Reeves the way I wanted to get Reeves meant destroying her in the process.

''I'm sorry, Gillian.''

''No, you're not.''

''Well, I wish I was sorry, at any rate. I just wish I didn't hate him so much.''

''And I just wish Annie didn't love you so much.''

She went to bed. I sat there a long time. After a while I blew out the lamp and just sat in the moonlight. I had some whiskey and I rolled two cigarettes and I sort of talked to my dead brothers the way you sort of talk to dead folks, and I thought of Annie in her white dress in the sunshine and I thought of sad Gillian, who'd been done nothing but wrong by men all her life.

It was near dawn when I went to bed and slid in beside her.

21

The next day, I fell back into my routine as husband and father and policeman.

Before work I went up the hill and knelt down by the deserted well. The day was gray and overcast. The wind, as I pulled the well cover back, was cold and biting. I could smell snow on the air.

Last night I'd dreamt that I'd run up the hill to the well only to find it empty. Behind me stood Lundgren and Mars. When I found that they'd taken the money, they'd started laughing, and then Lundgren had leaned over and pushed me down the well.

The rope still dangled from the spike. I reached down and gripped it and pulled the canvas money sack up the long dark hole.

I put the sack on the ground and greedily tore it open and reached inside.

I pulled up a handful of greenbacks and just stared at them momentarily. I gripped the money tight, as if I had my hands around Reeves' neck.

"You're destroying this family, Chase. That's what you're doing."

In the wind, I hadn't heard Gillian come up the hill. She stood no more than two feet behind me. She wore a shawl over her faded gingham dress. She looked old again, and scared and weary, and I tried hard not to hate myself for what I was doing.

"This money is going to save us, Gillian," I said, packing it all back up again, leaning to the well and feeding the rope down the long dark tunnel. I didn't let go until I'd tested the rope. Snug and firm. The spike held. The money was back in a safe place. I pulled the cover over the well and dusted my hands off and stood up.

I took her by the arms and tried to kiss her. She wouldn't let me. She just stood stiff. Her skin was covered with goose bumps from the icy wind.

She wouldn't look at me. I spoke to her profile, to her sweet little nose and her freckles and her tiny chin.

"All we need to do is wait a few months, and then we can leave town with all this money. Tell Hollister that one of your relatives died and left you a farm in Missouri or somewhere. Even if he suspects, he can't prove it. I'll wrap the money in bundles and put it in a trunk and send the trunk on ahead to wherever we decide to go."

When she finally turned and looked at me, she seemed sadder than I'd ever seen her.

"And won't that be a nice life for Annie, Chase? Watching her father scared all the time because somebody might find the money he stole?"

"I won't be scared, Gillian, because nobody will know except you and me. And it's not stolen money, anyway, not really—it's just what Reeves rightfully owes me."

"Listen to yourself, Chase," she said. "You've convinced yourself that what you're doing is right. But all you're doing is destroying this family. You wait and see. You wait and see."

She started crying, and then she was running down the hill, pulling her shawl tighter around her.

I started after her but decided there was no point. Not right now, anyway.

All I could do was stand there in the bitter wind, feeling like a kid who'd just been scolded. I wanted to speak up on my own behalf, but I knew better, knew that no matter what I said or how long I talked, straight and true Gillian would remain straight and true.

After a while I walked back down the hill to the house. Gillian was fixing stew at the stove. She didn't once turn around and look at me as I got into my police uniform, or say good-bye as I stood in the doorway and said, "I love you, Gillian. You and Annie are my life. And this is all going to work out. We're going to have the money and have a good life away from here. I promise you that, Gillian. I promise you that."

But there was just her back, her tired beaten shoulders, and her arm stirring the ladle through the stew.

22

When I got to town, the funeral procession was just winding its way up the hill to the graveyard. A lone man in a Union uniform walked behind the shiny black horse-drawn hearse, beating out a dirge on a drum.

I went to the police station, checked over the sheet listing the arrests thus far that day, checked to see if the new and more comfortable shoes I'd ordered had come in yet, and then started out the front door. There was still time for a cup of coffee at the restaurant before my rounds began.

As I walked to the front of the station, I felt various eyes on me.

A cop named Docey said, "Some of us were talkin' last night, Chase."

"Oh?"

"There were six of us talkin', and five of us voted that you should quit." He was leaning against the front door, a pudgy red-bearded man with red freckles on his white bald head. "We got enough problems without people thinkin' we're crooked."

"I didn't slip that key to the robbers, in case that's what you're talking about."

He grabbed me then. He pushed away from the door and took his big Irish hands and grabbed the front of

110

my uniform coat. I heard the two other cops grunt in approval.

I couldn't afford any more physical pain. I used my knee and I went right up straight and he went down fast and sure.

He rolled around on the floor clutching his groin and swearing. The other two started toward me but then realized that if Docey couldn't handle me—Docey being a mean mick ex-railroad man—they couldn't either.

I opened the front door, about to step out on the boardwalk into the bitter blustering day, and I saw her shiny black surrey pull up.

In her dark cape and royal-blue organdy dress, red hair caught beneath a small hat, Claire Hollister was not only beautiful, she was also exotic, like a frightened forest creature you see only once or twice a year for mere moments.

As she stepped down from the surrey, she nodded good day to me.

"Afternoon, ma'am."

"Afternoon." She smiled. "D-Did y-you h-happen t-to see that h-husband of m-mine in there?" As always, her sad eyes reflected her humiliation.

"I think he's still at the funeral, ma'am."

"Oh. W-Would y-you l-leave a n-note telling h-him I was h-here?"

"Sure."

She turned back to her surrey. As she seated herself and lifted the reins, I saw how sad her face was even in profile. I couldn't imagine why a woman like this— a woman I sensed was decent and honorable—would give herself to a man like Reeves. Sometimes I suspected I didn't know anything about women at all.

After she was gone, I went back inside. I had to pass

111

Docey and the other two cops, but they just scowled at me and let me go.

I wrote the chief a note and took it into his office. I started to set the note on his desk but then I noticed an envelope addressed to him. It bore the same handwriting as the note that had told him I was a jailbird.

I stood very still, staring at the envelope, making sure I was alone in the office, listening hard for any footsteps in the hallway.

I had to be quick. And I certainly couldn't risk reading it in here.

I snapped the envelope up, stuffed it inside my serge uniform coat, and walked straight out of the office and straight down the hallway and straight to the door, where Docey was still standing up and grimacing.

"You'll get yours, Chase, just you wait and goddamn see," he said.

Snow was still on the wind. The people on the street didn't dawdle now, they scurried like all other animals, trying to prepare themselves for the bitter winter soon to come. I imagined the general store, with its bacon and hams and coffee and cheeses and pickled fish and candy and tobacco and blankets and toys, was going to be doing a very good business the next few days as people set things in for the fury of winter.

I went over to the restaurant and ordered a cup of coffee. By the time the waitress came back with my steaming cup, I had already read the letter twice, and I sure didn't like what Reeves had written.

23

Dear Chief Hollister,

As an upright citizen of this town, I've warned you before about your man Chase. While everybody suspects he gave the robber the key that let him in the bank, nobody can prove it. Till now . . .

Ask Hartley, the night clerk at the Whitney, about the robbers and Chase meeting behind the hotel two nights before the robbery.

If he tells the truth, you'll see that Chase was in on this meeting all along.

So Reeves had got to Hartley, the night clerk at the hotel where Lundgren and Mars had been staying. Wouldn't take much to bribe a man like Hartley. Just as it wouldn't take much to convince Hollister of Hartley's story, that I had met with Lundgren and Mars to plan the robbery.

Even if I burned this particular letter, Reeves would send Hollister another one. And keep sending him letters until Hollister decided to put me behind bars . . . a perfect target for the lynch mob Reeves would quickly stir up.

I wanted to run. I thought about Mexico and warm blue waters and sandy yellow beaches and Gillian and Annie and I living in a fine stucco house. . . .

But if I ran now, it would be like signing a confession, admitting that I'd been part of the robbery.

I sipped coffee. I smoked a cigarette. I thought things through.

I had only one hope. I had to strike a bargain with Reeves.

"Yes?"

"Wondered if I could talk to you a minute, Chief."

"About what?"

"I might be a little late getting to today."

Hollister waved me into his office.

"By the way, your wife was here. I just wanted to make sure you got my note."

"I got it. Now what's this about being late?"

"Couple hours is all."

"For what?"

"Some personal things."

"Personal things, huh?"

"Not anything to do with the robbery, if that's what you're thinking."

He picked up his pipe. He'd been cleaning it with his pocketknife. Now he went back to it.

"You're not telling me the truth yet, Chase."

"I am. You just don't happen to believe the truth."

"You've got those jailhouse eyes, Chase. You think you look like every other man in this town, but you don't. Prison does something to people, and it sure as hell did something to you."

"I didn't help anybody rob that bank."

He put the pipe in his mouth and drew on it. There was a sucking sound in the empty bowl. "You could always turn them over."

"The robbers?"

114

"Lundgren and Mars are their names, in case you need help remembering."

"I don't know where they are."

"Uh-huh."

"I don't."

"Take the two hours." He sounded disgusted. "I don't know why you'd want to waste a fine wife and daughter the way you are."

"I'll be back by four-thirty."

"Don't hurry on my account. I'm getting damned tired of seeing your face, in fact."

24

Even on a cold drab day like this one, Reeves' Victorian house was impressive and sightly. I sat on my horse staring at it, trying not to notice that I was working up another fever and that my stomach was getting sick again.

Hanratty, the guard, appeared just when I expected him to, and leveled his carbine at me just when I was sure he would. He came out from behind the scrub pines, seated on a big bay.

"Nice uniform you got there, Chase. Maybe I could get Reeves to get me one like it."

"Maybe if you did an extra-good job, he just might do that."

Hanratty was bundled up inside a sheep-lined jacket, with his hat pulled down near his ears. He spat a stream of juice right near my horse's foreleg. "He'd be real happy to hear you went for your gun and I was forced to kill you. That's one way I could get me a uniform like that." He grinned. "Every time he works that wolf of his these days, he's always callin' out your name. And that goddamned wolf goes crazy, believe me. Crazy as all hell." He frowned. "Except the past couple days. Animal ain't hisself."

"All right if I go see Reeves?"

"It's your ass, son. He might put a couple holes in you."

I smiled. "I'm a policeman."

"Where you're concerned, I don't reckon that would make a whole lot of difference to him."

I rode up to the mansion and ground-tied my horse. Before going up the steps, I walked over to the side of the house and looked at the wolf in his cage.

The wolf, crouched on the ground, watching me carefully, wailed out something that resembled a song, a wolf song, I guessed. I'd never heard anything like it. It was angry for sure, but even more, it was sad.

I walked a few feet closer to the large, oblong cage that stank of feces and raw decaying meat, and I saw that Hanratty hadn't been exaggerating about the wolf's anger, either.

He got up on all fours, let out another terrible piercing sound, and then flung himself at the cage. His eyes burned with the same yellow glow I'd seen that night he'd killed my brother.

His bared teeth dripped with drool, and his entire body trembled as he slammed again and again and again into the wire, trying to tear through the wall to get to me. The reverberating wire made a tinny kind of music.

I had my gun in hand and ready, just in case.

"Maybe I'll put you in there with him," said a voice behind me, the words accompanied by the nudge of cold metal against the back of my neck. "What the hell're you doing here, anyway, Chase?"

"Talk a deal."

"Deal?" Reeves laughed. "What the hell's that supposed to mean?"

"Let's go inside and I'll tell you."

He wore a riding costume, a fancy eastern riding costume, one of those things with jodhpurs and knee-length riding boots. He was real pretty.

"You're really serious, aren't you?" he said.

"Yes."

He laughed again. "Then you're a crazy bastard, Chase. A crazy, crazy bastard. Men like me don't make deals with men like you."

"If you ever want to see any of that bank money again, Reeves, you'd better invite me inside."

The wolf was exhausted. He'd spent himself and lay now panting, his entire body heaving with hot breath, and making those funny sounds again.

"Something's wrong with your wolf," I said.

"You and that goddamned Hanratty. The wolf's just got some kind of bug is all. Wolves get bugs just the same as humans. If he was really sick, he wouldn't be able to throw himself against the cage that way."

"Be sure to wipe that mud off your boots before you go inside," Reeves said. "I don't want some hayseed tracking up my good hardwood floors."

"I take it you're inviting me inside," I said, but when I turned around, Reeves was already up near the front porch, as if he didn't ever want to be seen with me, not even on his own land.

I turned back to the keening wolf and listened to his terrible sounds echo off the surrounding hills, like a distress call of some kind that nobody was answering.

"You have two minutes, and then I want you the hell off my property."

We were in his office, the same one where he'd cold-cocked me that day.

"I have your money," I said. He was behind his desk. He hadn't invited me to sit down.

"I'm well aware of the fact that you have my money."

"But I'm willing to make a deal."

"You heard what I said about deals, Chase."

"You get half and I get half."

"I get half of my own money and you get the other half? That sounds like a hell of a deal, all right."

"Otherwise you get nothing."

"We'll see who gets nothing, Chase. This isn't over yet."

I sat down. He didn't look especially happy about it. "You want to hear about it?"

I could tell he did but he didn't want to say he did—he didn't want to give any sign that I was in control here—so I went on anyway.

"You get ahold of Ev Hollister and tell him you made a mistake about me. Tell him that you forgot that one day you hung your coat up over at the Whitney while you were having lunch, and when you got back, you found your wallet missing. The bank key was in there. But while you went to the manager to complain, somebody slipped your wallet back into your coat."

"In other words, somebody had a duplicate key made?"

"Exactly."

"And why would he believe this?"

"Because it's you talking. Because you're a prominent citizen and he'd have no reason to suspect you're lying."

"And for this I get half my money back?"

"Right."

"And what do you get, Chase?"

"I get half the money and I get a chance to ease me and my family out of this town without this cloud hanging over me. I'll buy a farm in Missouri and disappear for the rest of my life with Gillian and Annie."

"Every jailbird's dream."

"I'm tired of your sarcasm, Reeves."

He smirked. "A jailbird sits in his cell and dreams up all these sweet little stories about how good life will be after he pulls just one more job." He leaned forward in his seat. "I should put a bullet in your face right here and right now." His anger was overtaking him now. He started spitting when he spoke. "You've got my money, you stupid hayseed asshole, and I'm going to take it back and you're going to regret ever having anything to do with me."

He waved his hand, spitting and glaring, blood spreading across his cheeks. "Now get the hell out of here."

"I figured out a peaceful way to end all this," I said. "I thought you'd want to listen."

He said nothing. Just glared.

I stood and picked up my hat and walked out of his den and down the hall, my bootheels loud in the silence, and out the front door.

I put my hat on and watched the wolf a moment. He was still crying, still that high mournful call, and still crouching, as if exhausted—until he saw me . . . and then he was up on all fours and leaping into the air and hurtling himself against the cage.

"He sure don't like you," an old Indian cleaning woman said, as she beat a rug against the porch railing.

"I guess he doesn't," I said.

On the way out, Hanratty waved to me and called, "Good to see you're still alive." I waved and rode on.

I just kept thinking of what Reeves had said, how every jailbird sits in his cell and thinks of how pretty things will be after he pulls that final job. Not till the very moment he'd said that had I ever thought of myself as a jailbird—just as a kid who'd gotten himself in some trouble, was all—but in his hard, bitter words I'd recognized myself. And now I felt every bit the hayseed he'd said I was. Trying to make a deal with him had been very foolish.

After a few more days, I'd gather up Gillian and Annie and the money, and in the middle of the night we'd light out and never be seen by any of these folks again. . . .

25

The rain started just after dinner time. Except for the light in the saloon windows, the stores and streets were dark as I made my rounds, trying doors, checking alleys, peering into storage shacks.

I was starting down Main, past three of the rowdier saloons, when I saw the two drunken miners weaving down the street toward me. They were laughing and stumbling their way home to warm houses and irritated wives and disappointed children.

Then they saw who I was and stopped and one of them said, ''There's that sonofabitch.''

''Who?''

''Goddamn cop who was in on that goddamn bank robbery.''

''No shit?''

''Where they killed the poor goddamned clerk with a goddamned double-barreled shotgun.''

''Poor sumbitch.''

By now I was abreast of them, making my way through the cold and the night and the lashing rain. They were too drunk to notice the downpour, or care about it, anyway.

There wasn't much I could do about them not liking me, the two drunks. I'd planned on taking their abuse and walking on by. I'd feel sorry for myself a few minutes and then the whole thing would be over.

Then the first drunk hit me.

I hadn't been expecting it and I didn't have time to do anything about it.

His punch came out of the gloom and struck me right on the jaw.

He'd hit me hard enough to daze me. There was pain and there was an even deeper darkness, and then I felt a second punch slam into my stomach.

It should have brought me down, that punch. It drove deep into my belly right below the ribs and it was expert enough and vicious enough to wind me for the moment.

But then rage and frustration took over. Suddenly this drunk became the whole town, everybody who smirked about me, everybody who whispered.

I threw down my nightstick, not wanting to make this an official act in any way, and without even being able to see yet, connected with a strong right to the drunk's face.

"Hey!" yelled the second drunk, as if defending myself was against some unwritten code.

But I didn't even slow down. I just kept punching. I even got a knee straight up between the first drunk's legs, and when he started to buckle, I grabbed him by the hair and started hitting him at will with my right fist.

By now I could see. The guy was bloody, though the rain did a good job of washing him up. He hadn't been intimidated by my uniform, but his friend was. He stood three feet away and called me names.

At first I wasn't aware of the crowd surrounding us, not until there were twenty people or so. They'd drifted down from the taverns, animals who could smell blood on the wind, animals whose taste for violence was never sated, miners, merchants, cowboys, drifters—it was a taste and thrill that cut across all lines of class and intelligence and color. Most men, and a sad number of women, loved watching other men hurt each other.

And I was hurting him, hurting him bad, and I couldn't stop. If anything, I was piling more and more punches into his body. The crowd was with me now, frenzied, caught up in my rhythms as I slammed punches first to the head then to the chest then to the belly, the same pattern again and again. He was bleeding so badly, his blood was flying across my own face.

"That's enough, Chase!"

At first the voice seemed far away and not quite recognizable. Familiar, yet . . .

And so I kept on swinging and slugging and—

And then, too late, I recognized the voice and I saw him, peripherally, step up next to me and raise his own nightstick and bring it down and—

And then there was just the eternal cosmic night, cold and dark, not life yet not quite death, either. Just pain and—blankness.

The crowd noise grew distant—and then faded entirely. . . .

I didn't get my eyes open right away. Couldn't. The pain across the back of my head was too considerable.

I became aware that my arms were stretched out behind me and my wrists were bound together. I became aware that my ankles were also bound. I became aware of some other presence near me. I had to open my eyes. Had to.

I almost smiled. He was treating me as a respected guest and he didn't even know it. None of his men ever got to see the inside of the room where Ev Hollister worked over his prisoners. But now Ev Hollister was letting me see it for myself.

"You were out a long time," he said.

He sat in a straight-backed chair directly across from the one I was sitting in.

"Afraid I tapped you a little harder than I meant to," he said.

There were dark brown splatters all over the wall, the dried blood of the prisoners he'd worked over in his time. There were also dents and nicks and small holes in the wall. When he got done punching the prisoners, he sometimes liked to throw them around the room. Everybody likes a little variety in his life.

I brought my eyes back to Hollister.

"You look pissed, Chase. Real pissed."

"Why'd you bring me into this room? I'm not a prisoner."

He smiled. It was a drunken smile, pleasing but crooked and not quite coordinated properly. "You're not a prisoner yet, you mean, Chase. This whole town's just like that miner who swung on you. They hate you, Chase, and they hold you responsible for the clerk's death and they're putting a lot of pressure on me to arrest you whether I've got evidence or not. These are simple folks, Chase, they're not like you and me with our fine respect for the written law." He tried to smile about empty, high-minded words, but what came out was a smirk.

I decided I might as well tell him. Maybe it was what he'd been wanting all along, anyway. "I'm planning to clear out in the next few days. Gillian and Annie and me. Gone for good."

"Well," he said, "now that's a damned sensible idea."

"So all your troubles will be over."

"The next few days?"

"So how about untying me?"

"You and your wife and daughter?"

"Right."

"As far away as you can get with no plans to ever come back?"

"That's the plan."

He stood up. The crooked smile was back. So was the drunken glaze of the eyes. He walked the four steps between my chair and his, and then he backhanded me so hard I went over backward, cracking my head on the floor.

I tried to struggle back up but it was no use. Lying on my back and tied up made me vulnerable to anything he wanted to do. But the fall had loosened the rope on my wrists.

He kicked me hard in the ribs.

The pain hadn't even had time to register properly before he walked around the chair and kicked me hard in the other rib, the one that I'd bruised a while back.

I closed my eyes and coasted on the blackness and the physical grief spreading across my rib cage and up into my chest and arms. Every few minutes, I'd become aware of my sore throat again. . . .

"Where are those two peckers?" he said.

I didn't want to give him another excuse to kick me. I answered right away. "I don't know."

"Like hell you don't, Chase. You stick up a bank with two men and you don't know where they are?"

"I don't. I'm telling you the truth."

"Then you've got the money, don't you?"

"No."

"Bullshit."

"Honest, Chief, I—"

He kicked me again. This was enough to shrivel my

126

scrotum into the size of a walnut and to send tears streaming down my cheeks. The toe of his boot had found the exact spot where the doc had bandaged my rib.

"Where's the money?"

"Don't . . . know."

"You sonofabitch."

And I could sense it, the frenzy, the way I was sure all his other prisoners had been able to sense it. When he was sober, he was a decent, humane man who ran an honest police department and had a genuine regard for the people he served.

But when he drank . . .

This time he walked around in front of me and looked straight down.

"You know where I'm going to kick you this time?"

"Please don't. Please." I didn't care how I sounded. I just didn't want any more pain.

"Then you tell me, Chase. You tell me where those men are and where that money is or I swear you won't get out of this room alive."

"I don't know. I really don't."

My groin wasn't all that easy a target, what with my ankles bound and all, but his boot toe was unerring and he found the spot with very little trouble.

I screamed. I tried praying, but all that came out was curses, and I tried biting my lip, but I bit down so hard I filled my mouth with blood.

And he kicked me again.

Almost instinctively, I kept working my hands free from the ropes behind me. But even if my hands were free, he had a gun and a nightstick and—

"You tell me, Chase, you tell me where those men are and that money is."

My body was cold with sweat. My face was swollen

from the punches of the miner. My ribs and groin hurt so much I was starting to drift into unconsciousness. . . .

"I'm giving you five seconds, Chase."

He was raising his boot. He was picking his spot.

"Five seconds, Chase."

"Please, Chief," I said again, and it wasn't even me speaking now, it was the scared little boy I'd been all the time I was growing up. "Please don't, Chief."

"Three seconds."

His foot came up even higher.

"Two seconds, Chase."

Oh and he was enjoying it, seeing me writhe on the floor, hearing me whimper.

"You sonofabitch," he said.

And was just starting to lift his leg when—

Somebody banged on the door.

"Chief, Chief, you'd better get out here."

He was angry, Ev Hollister was. It was as if somebody had interrupted him having sex at the crucial moment.

"What the hell is it, Fenady?"

"Those two men we been looking for? Lundgren and Mars?"

Hollister's face changed. Anger gone, replaced with curiosity.

"What about them?"

"Somebody found them in a field the other side of Chase's cabin. And brought them in."

"They're dead?"

"Yeah. Back-shot."

Hollister smiled down at me. "Didn't know where they were, eh, Chase?"

This time he didn't give any warning. He just took two steps to the right, where he could get a better angle, and then brought his toe down swiftly and surely into my rib cage.

Fenady probably winced when he heard me scream. Even the cops who hate prisoners hate to hear human beings worked over the way Hollister works them over.

Hollister looked down at me. "I'm going out there and check those men over. When I come back, I want you to tell me what you did with the money after you killed those two men."

"But I—"

I'd started to say that I hadn't back-shot anybody, that Reeves had done it and made it look as if I had, the way he made it look as if my key had been used in the robbery.

But what was the point of talking now? Hollister wouldn't believe me no matter how many times I told him the truth.

He went over to the door, unlocked it and went out.

26

The ropes slid off my wrists with no trouble. But bending down to uncinch my ankles, I felt nauseous and dizzy. Because of the beating, the sickness was getting worse.

Through the door I could hear the commotion far down the hall, in the front office.

As I started unwrapping the rope again, I thought of how long I'd suffered at Reeves' hands. Most of my adult life he'd ruled me in one way or another. I'd been a kid when I helped pull the robbery he set me up for. And now he'd convinced Hollister that I'd back-shot the two men who had allegedly been my partners.

I reached the door, eased it open, peered down the hall and started on tiptoes down the stairs and toward the back door. I reached the ground floor and continued to tiptoe down the hall and—

I got two steps away from the doorknob when somebody shouted, "Hey!"

I turned and saw Krause, a big red-faced German cop, lunging for me with his nightstick.

He swung but I ducked. His stick hit the door above my head so hard that it snapped in two.

I knew I had no chance other than to grab the knob, throw the door open and dive into the night outside.

Krause swore and lumbered toward me, but his jaw

intersected with the edge of the door just as it was opening. He was knocked to his knees. I turned around, kicked him in the throat, and then pushed him over backward. As I hit the alley, he was swearing at me in German.

All I could do was run. I had no idea where I was going.

I came to the head of an alley and stopped, leaning out from the shadows to get a look at the street. Mrs. Hollister had pulled her fancy black surrey over by the general store and was watching all the men running in the street. Apparently all the shouting over the death of Lundgren and Mars had brought her out of the house. They lived near the downtown area.

I ducked back into the alley, pausing to catch my breath, then I started running again.

I went two blocks and then collapsed against a building, my breath coming in hot raw gasps.

There was moonlight and the deep shadows of the alley and the sweet smell of newly sawn lumber from a nearby store that had recently gone up.

And behind me I could hear the shouts. "He escaped! Chase escaped!"

They would come looking for me now, the human equivalents of bloodhounds, and there wouldn't be just policemen, but eager private citizens, too, eager for some sport.

I pushed away from the wall and started staggering down the alley. When I reached the last building, I pressed myself against it and peeked around the corner.

They already had torches lit, and they were coming toward me three abreast. They hadn't seen me yet but it would be only moments before they did.

I heard noise at the far end of the alley and turned to

find three men with torches approaching. They would see me any time now.

I looked frantically around the alley. All I could find was a large barrel in which the general store threw food that had spoiled. Even on a cold night like this one, the contents of the barrel reeked. In the summer it had been noisy with flies twenty-four hours a day.

I had no choice. I jerked open the lid and crawled inside, hoping that the shadows would hide me sufficiently from the oncoming men.

I sank deep into a fetid, swampy mixture of rotted produce. For a long time I had to hold my breath. I was afraid I'd vomit and the men would certainly hear me.

Their voices and their footsteps came closer.

The two groups met in the alley, near where I crouched in the barrel.

"I never did like that bastard," one man said. "Just something about him."

"Strange is what he is," another said. "You ever get a good look in sunlight at how scarred up his face is underneath that beard? Very strange how a man would come to get scars like that. Kind've gives me the willies."

"Enough talk," a third man said, sounding important. "You three take the Fourth Street alleys and we'll take Third Street. No way he could've gotten out of town yet."

"Oh, he's here somewhere all right," said another man.

As one of them turned around, he nudged the barrel. I froze. I had the sense that they could all hear my heartbeat like an Indian drum deep in the forest late at night.

"He could be hidin' right here," the man said. "In

this alley. Maybe we should check it out before we go over to Third Street.''

"Hell, Hawkins, look around. Where the hell would he hide?''

"Right over there in that privy, for one thing.''

Another man laughed. "Yep, he's sittin' in there ta-kin' a crap and readin' a Sears catalog.''

More laughter.

"Well, it sure wouldn't hurt to check it out,'' Haw-kins said, sounding petulant.

"Be my guest.''

Hawkins walked away. Ten, maybe fifteen paces. The privy was right behind the back door of the restaurant halfway down the alley.

"Stick your head down that hole in there and see if he's hidin' down there!'' one of the men said, laughing.

There was no response from Hawkins, none I could hear anyway.

Bugs and mites were crawling on me, species that apparently didn't relent in November weather. I wanted to scratch myself but there was no room, and anyway doing so would probably make too much noise.

And then the lid was lifted.

This time my heart didn't start pounding. It stopped.

I sank as far down into the garbage as I could go and watched as a plump white hand dangled over the rim of the barrel.

One of the men was dropping his cigar in here.

"What a goddamn smell,'' he said. "All that pro-duce.''

"Had a little girl in South Dakota who smelled just like it.'' The other man laughed.

The lid was still off. The man's hand was still dan-gling, his cigar butt looking like a red-eyed snake.

And then he tossed it.

The lighted end of the butt struck me right in the forehead.

The pain was instant and considerable. I gritted my teeth. I made fists. I wanted to curse. But no way I could indulge myself.

The lid closed.

Hawkins returned. "Nobody there."

"Gee, what a surprise."

"Well, he coulda been there," Hawkins said.

"Yeah, and so coulda Jesus H. Christ himself."

"C'mon," said the third man. "Let's get moving. I'd like to find that sonofabitch myself. Show him that without that fancy blue uniform to protect him, he ain't jack shit."

I waited five minutes, during which time I had a pretty crazy thought. What if they actually knew I was in the barrel and had just snuck away a few feet and waited while I climbed out?

I would climb out of the barrel and they would open fire and I'd be dead. A nice, legal execution, something to talk about in saloons and taverns for the next twenty years.

I slid the lid open.

I reached up and grabbed the rim of the deep barrel.

Above me I saw the cold starry sky.

I pushed myself up, tatters of garbage clinging to me, and started to climb out of the barrel.

So far, so good, but I knew that my biggest problem was ahead of me.

How was I going to escape a town filled with torch-bearing posse members?

I scrambled from the barrel and immediately hid myself in the shadows again.

What was I going to do now?

And then I saw the buggy, the shiny black buggy, and without any thought at all I started running toward it.

27

The Hollister woman wasn't expecting me.

I ran from the mouth of the alley straight at her surrey, my toe landing on the vehicle's metal step while I dove down beside her feet.

She started to scream, but all I had to say was one thing. "If you don't help me, Mrs. Hollister, I'll tell your husband about you and Reeves."

She'd been all set to cry out, her mouth forming an O, but at mention of Reeves the scream died in her throat.

"I want to go out Orely Road, and fast," I said.

She seemed confused, as if she hadn't quite recovered from the shock of seeing me jump into her surrey. But then intelligence returned to her eyes and she gathered the reins tighter, made a wide turn with horse and surrey, and started us on our way out of town. The animal was running at a good steady clip.

I kept watching her face to see if she was trying to signal the men who were running past, sounding excited as hayseeds at a county fair.

The ride, with me all curled up at her feet, was bumpy. Every time we hit a rut, she kicked me in my rib with the pointed toe of her high-button shoe. I could smell horseshit and axle grease. I wanted Gillian and Annie in my arms.

The flickering street lamps fell away after a time, as did the sound of running feet slapping the hard dirt road. Even the high, charged shouts of the eager posse.

After a while I raised myself up enough to look out at the rutted road. Moonlight showed a narrow stage road with ice shining in the potholes, and all around an autumnal mountainous land touched with glowing frost. Bears would be sleeping deep in winter caves by now, and kids would be asking for extra blankets.

I swung up from the floor and sat down next to her.

"H-How did you know about R-Reeves?" she said, and when she stuttered, I felt ashamed of myself. I had no right to judge this woman the way I had.

"Forget I said anything. I'm not fit to pass judgment on you, Mrs. Hollister."

We didn't say anything for a time. The only sound was the crack of hooves against icy road.

I sat and watched the frozen night go by, the jet silhouettes of mountains against the darker jet of the sky, the hoarfrost quarter moon, the silver-blue underbellies of clouds . . .

"Y-You d-don't know what my h-husband's l-like when he d-drinks."

She sounded miserable and I had to stop her. "I shouldn't have said that, Mrs. Hollister. Really. I don't have any right to judge you."

She started shaking her head from side to side, reliving an old grief. "I'm a s-sinful w-woman, M-Mr. Chase. I'm a h-harlot."

We fell into silence again.

Then, "I t-told him t-today that I d-don't p-plan on s-seeing him a-anymore."

I reached over and touched her shoulder. "You should have respect for yourself, Mrs. Hollister. You could do a lot better than Reeves, believe me."

And Gillian could do a lot better than me.

She didn't say anything the rest of the way.

When the road turned westward, I took the reins from her and brought the horse to a halt.

"I hope things go right for you, Mrs. Hollister. You seem like a decent woman."

She smiled and leaned over. I thought she was going to kiss me. Instead she just touched my cheek with long fingers. Tenderly.

I jumped down and started walking to the edge of the hill, from which I could look down into the valley and see our house.

What I saw was the old farm wagon that Gillian kept in back. It was loaded down with clothes and furnishings. Gillian and Annie sat up on the seat. They'd hitched up the horse and were just now pulling out of the yard.

The sickness was getting worse all the time, but I ran anyway, ran faster than I ever had in my life.

"Gillian!" I cried into the night. "Gillian!"

28

By the time I got near the wagon, it had climbed the hill and was just starting down the road.

As I came close, out of breath, my legs threatening to crumple at any moment, I heard the clang of pots and pans as the wagon bounced along the road.

I fell.

I was twenty feet at most from the wagon, and I went straight down, my toe having stumbled over a pothole.

I stayed on my hands and knees for two or three minutes, like a dog trying to regain his strength. The vast night was starry and cold; the clang of pots and pans faded in the distance; and all I could smell was the hot sweat of my sickness.

After a time I got to my feet. But I promptly sank back down. Too weak.

I stayed down till I lost sight of the wagon in the moonlight far ahead. It had rounded a curve and was now behind a screen of jack pines. By this time the clank of kitchen implements was almost endearing, like a memory of Annie's smile.

All of a sudden I was having trouble swallowing, taking saliva down in gulps. Part of the sickness, I knew.

I started off walking and slowly began running. I had to catch the wagon. Had to.

* * *

By the time I caught up with them, the fever was so bad I was partially blind, a darkness falling across my vision every minute or so.

This time Annie heard me. She stood up in the wagon and turned around and saw me.

The last thing I heard, just before I pitched forward in the sandy road, was Annie's scream.

Darkness.

Squeak of wagon; clop of horse on hard-packed road; faint scent of perfume in the bed of the wagon.

Gillian.

"You're going to see that doctor in the morning, and I'm going to personally take you."

"I can't see anything."

"You just rest."

"My eyes—"

"Rest."

"Where are we?"

"Annie's taking us back home. She convinced me to give you another chance."

"Gillian—"

"And you're going to turn that money over and you're going to face whatever punishment you've got coming, and then we're going to be a real family for the first time in our lives."

She leaned down. All I could smell in the darkness was her soft sweet scent. She kissed me on the forehead, a mother's kiss.

"Sleep, now. We'll be home soon."

And so the old farm wagon tossed and squeaked down the road, the horse plodding but true, Annie talking to him most of the time, imitating the way adults talked to their wagon horses.

After a time the darkness was gone and I could see

the stars again, and I wondered what it would be like to live on one of them, so far away from human grief. But they probably had their own griefs, the people on those stars, ones just as bad as ours.

29

She got me out of my sweat-soaked clothes and put on water for hot tea. She put me in bed and had Annie come in and stand over me while she gathered up more blankets. By now the chills were pretty bad.

"Mommy said that in a little while things will be all right again and you won't be in trouble anymore."

The bedroom was lit by moonlight, and Annie, one half of her face silver, the other half shadow, looked like a painting.

"That's right, honey."

"She said some men would probably come after you. Chief Hollister, she said. Doesn't he like you anymore?"

Gillian was back with more blankets. Annie helped her spread them over me.

Annie started talking again. I held her small hand in mine and tried to say something in return but I didn't have the strength. My throat was raw, my head hurt, every bone in my body ached, and I was having a hard time making sense of words.

I slept.

At first I thought it was part of a dream, the way the horses thundered toward me from the distant hill. I often had dreams where I was being pursued by fierce men on fiercer horses.

But then I heard Gillian saying, "They're coming down the hill, Chase. The posse."

Instinct took over. In moments I was out of bed, grabbing dry clothes and a jacket and throwing them on, picking up my .45 and a fancy bone-handled bowie knife I'd bought on a lark before going to prison.

Gillian watched me. "I thought maybe you'd turn yourself in, instead of running away."

As I buttoned the fleece-lined jacket, I said, "I don't want them to take me into town tonight, Gillian. Not with everybody worked up the way they are. I've seen two lynchings in my life and they were both real scary."

"Where are you going?"

"I'm going to get the money and then wait till the posse leaves."

"But they'll find you."

"Not where I'm going to hide."

The horses were closer, closer.

She came into my arms and we held each other. And then I took off, moving quickly to the back door. In moments I was out in the cold night again.

I peeked around the corner of the cabin and saw them—

Six horses coming down the dark November wind—

Six riders on the hill, three bearing torches with flames that crackled and flapped like pennants in the wind, and three with carbines already drawn from leather scabbards.

Ready to make the descent, encircle the cabin, and drag me out to meet their justice.

30

The wind was raw as I dropped to my knees up there where the deserted well lay. A dark cloud passed across the moon, and for a brief time all color was blanched from the land, and the rocks and plains and mountains did not seem to be of earth at all, but some strange land from my prison nightmares.

I jerked the lid from the well and plunged my hand down into the chilly darkness below. All I could feel was the cold, empty blackness of the grave.

They would be coming up here looking for me, the posse would. There was only one place I could hide.

I wound the top of the rope tight around one of the large rocks at the mouth of the well. I tugged it several times, making sure that it was strong enough to hold me. The rock must have weighed two hundred pounds. It would be fine. But the rope was frayed . . .

I didn't have any choice.

I grabbed the rope end, climbed up over the rocks around the opening of the well and started my descent, feeding myself rope as I went.

Dirt and small rocks from the sides of the well fell to the water below, making a hollow splashing sound when they hit.

If I fell, nobody would ever find me. I'd hit my head

or drown or I'd be trapped down there and freeze to death.

I kept on moving down, inch by inch. I kept thinking of sad Gillian there at the last moment . . . wanting only the one thing I couldn't give her . . . wanting to be safe from my hatred of Reeves.

There was a sour smell just as I got so low that darkness took me entirely. Gases . . .

Far up above me I saw a portion of the well opening and a piece of cold midnight sky.

I was tightening my grip on the rope when another wave of blindness overwhelmed me. All I could do was hold on and hope it would pass.

And it was there, blind, suspended halfway down a well, that I whispered the word to myself, the word I'd been avoiding the past few days. . . .

Then the voices, harsh male voices on the witch's wind down from the mountains.

Coming up the hill—

Looking for me.

"Here's a well!" somebody shouted.

They would find the cover off and put a torch down into the darkness and find me.

"The hell with the well! Look over there in that stand of jack pines."

This was Ev Hollister's voice. He was leading his own posse.

I went lower and lower in case they came back and looked down the well. They wouldn't have much trouble finding me, if they wanted to look. It was a very shallow well.

The heels of my boots touched water.

I stopped my descent, just hung there listening to the voices of the posse fade in and out on the wind.

Obviously they'd given up; the voices were moving back down the hill, in the direction of the house.

I just kept thinking of that word I'd been so afraid to say the past couple of days. . . .

I felt the top of the money sack.

I grasped it and began to pull it up and—

The rope started to give at the very top.

Even as I hung there, I could feel it begin to fray and weaken.

In a moment I would be dropped into the water and entombed forever . . . terrible fever pictures came to me. I would be prisoner down here forever, till I was only white bones for greasy black snakes to wind in and out of, and for the rats to perch on as, crimson-eyed, they surveyed the well. . . . I felt as if I was suffocating.

Distant starlight in the midnight sky was my only guide now.

I stabbed my heels against the shale walls of the well. Propped up this way, I could at least keep from being pitched into the water.

With one hand dredging up the money sack, and my boot heels digging into the wall . . .

I started to climb.

All I could hope was that Hollister and his men would be gone by the time I reached the top.

I just kept looking straight up at the bright indifferent stars above. In prison I'd read about how many worlds our stars shine on, so many that our little world hardly matters at all.

Even with everybody on our planet screaming, nobody in the universe could hear us anyway. . . .

I knew I was getting sicker all the while, my mind fixing on things like astronomy, my bones and joints aching so bad I could hardly keep a grip on the rope or the sack.

And every few feet the rope would fray a little more and I would feel the tug and jerk as it threatened to tear apart completely . . .

But I kept on climbing.

I have no idea how long it took me.

By the time I reached the top, I was gasping for breath.

I threw the bag over the top of the well first. It landed on the frosty earth with a satisfying thump.

And then I wrapped both hands in the rope and climbed the rest of the way up, cutting my hands on hemp and jagged rock alike, till hot blood flowed from my palms.

But I didn't care. . . .

I lay for long minutes on the hard cold earth. The chill air felt cool and cleansing on my fevered skin.

I got to my feet, grabbed the money sack, and started walking back up the hill.

Beyond the hill were Gillian and Annie. . . .

When I reached the other side, I swung wide eastward, so I could come up behind a copse of jack pines. From here I could see the front of the cabin clearly . . . yet I was so well-hidden that nobody could see me.

Five riders with torches sat horses. The wind-whipped flames made the faces of the men look like burnished masks.

There was a sixth horse, its saddle empty, standing ground-tied. Where was its rider?

Gillian stood in the doorway—Annie clinging to her like a very small child—talking to the men.

Suddenly a man came from the cabin. He was toting a Winchester. He'd obviously been searching the place, seeing if I was hiding there.

It was Hollister. He got back up on his horse.

There was more talk between the men and Gillian, the words lost in the midnight wind.

And then they left. Abruptly. Just turned their horses and headed westward, the light from their torches diminishing as they reached the edge of the great forest, where they likely thought I'd gone.

Gillian and Annie stood outside the cabin for long moments watching the men disappear into the great pines.

And then, just as I was about to call out for Gillian, I felt the darkness overwhelm me again, felt all my strength go and my body begin to sink to the ground.

Once again I slept. . . .

31

The prison dreams came again . . . watching the teenager drown as the old con held him under . . . listening to the screams of the men as whips lashed their backs . . . seeing a wolf silhouetted against the full golden moon as he stood on the hill overlooking the prison. . . .

Even in sleep my teeth chattered from the cold of my skin and baked in the heat of my insides.

I wanted Gillian . . . I wanted Annie. . . .

And then the scream.

At first I counted it as part of my nightmares. Only when its intensity and pitch were sustained did I realize that it was Annie screaming.

I crawled to my feet, covered with pine, so dry I could barely part my lips. I felt at my side for my .45. Still there.

Annie kept on screaming.

I staggered across the clearing.

The cabin was dark but the front door was flung wide, and there in the doorway I saw him crouching—

The wolf.

His yellow eyes gleamed and across his face were dark damp streaks of—blood.

I tried to understand what had gone on here. . . .

Reeves had come here to get the money and had brought his wolf along with him.

He growled but moved cautiously away so I could go inside.

I went into the cabin.

And saw Annie at the entrance to our bedroom door.

Her flannel gown had been shredded by wolf claws, and she lay bloody and unconscious, half propped up against the door frame, her golden hair darkened by splashes of her own blood.

I stumbled toward her, paying no attention to the snarl and growl of the wolf behind me. I reached the door and looked in on the bed and there—

Gillian had not been so lucky. She had been eviscerated.

The wolf had ripped most of her clothes off and had then torn open her throat and stomach.

I struggled toward her, fell next to her on the bed, felt for a pulse I knew my fingers would never feel.

Gillian—

She looked like a fawn that had been attacked by a ravenous predator, and when I put my fingers to her lips . . . she was already getting cold. I must have been out longer than I realized.

I took out my .45 and went over to Annie.

Beneath her bloody flesh I felt a pulse in both neck and wrist, and I snatched her up like an infant and carried her in the crook of my left arm.

I kept my right hand free to use the gun.

The gray lobo still crouched in the front doorway. A growl rumbling up its chest and throat. Waiting for me.

I raised my .45, sighted, began to squeeze the trigger, and—

He sprang.

He was so heavy yet so fast that he knocked my gun away before I could shoot accurately.

Two, three shots went wild in the darkness, the flame red-yellow in the shadows.

And then the wolf was on top of me, Annie having rolled out of my grasp as I was knocked to the floor.

He was all muscle beneath the blood-soaked gray fur, all madness in yellow eyes and blood-dripping mouth.

All I knew was to protect my throat. Once his teeth or claws reached it . . .

I rolled left and right, right and left, trying to keep him off balance until I could roll away from him completely.

By now I was beyond pain, he had ripped and bitten me so often, first across the forehead and then across the chest, and then across the belly, heat and saliva and urgent, pounding body slamming into me again and again.

And finally I started to feel myself give up. No more strength; maybe not even any more determination. Too much pain and weakness. Overwhelming . . .

And then I heard, as if I were unconscious and dreaming again, a terrified but very angry voice saying, "Leave my daddy alone! Leave my daddy alone!" She was awake now, and had found my .45, which she held up with surprising confidence.

And then there were two huge booming shots in the gloom, and the sudden cry of a wolf seriously wounded, and then the cry of a young child as she collapsed again to the floor.

The wolf, shocked, bleeding badly already from the bullets in his chest and stomach—the wolf began to crawl out the front door, crying so sadly even I felt a moment of sorrow for it.

I slowly got to my feet and crawled over to Annie.

I took her to me and held her, and at first I couldn't tell if the crying was hers or mine.

"I'm sorry I brought all this on, Annie," I said, "your mother was right. I shouldn't have tried to get Reeves."

But she was unconscious in my arms, and my words were wasted.

And then I heard the wet snort of a horse near the front door.

I lay Annie down carefully, grabbed my .45 and ran to the doorway.

In the moonlit grass before the door, Reeves knelt next to the wounded wolf, stroking the animal as it crouched, growling, at the sight of me.

To Reeves's left his horse stood waiting for him. And then—

Reeves brought his right hand up—

I barely had time to duck back inside before the bullet tore away an inch of wood from the door frame.

Two more shots, quickly. And then silence.

Before I could crawl back to the door frame, I heard Reeves swing up on his horse—saddle leather creaking—and start to ride away.

By the time I reached the door frame and steadied my hand enough to squeeze off some shots, Reeves was fast becoming a silhouette on the hill—fast-retreating horse and rider with the gray lobo running alongside.

I fired twice but only to sate my rage. From this distance, I had no hope of hitting him.

I forced myself to ladle up some water for Annie. The mere smell of it still nauseated me.

I got her on the floor in the kitchen, dragged out a blanket, and propped her head up on a pillow I'd taken from the back of the rocking chair.

Every few moments I felt her wrist for a pulse. I had to keep reassuring myself that she was alive.

I raised her head and gave her water. Her eyes fluttered open but remained so only briefly.

I was just starting to examine her wounds when I heard, on the distant hill, the sound of a rider coming fast.

Reeves. Come back for the fight that was inevitable.

I kissed Annie on the forehead and then grabbed my gun and moved to the doorway, keeping to the shadows so he couldn't see me.

As I leaned against the wall, waiting for him, I heard Annie moan. She needed a doctor, and quickly. After I finished Reeves . . .

The rider stopped short a few hundred feet from the cabin. Eased off his saddle. Ground-tied his beast. Grabbed his carbine from the scabbard. Crouched and started moving toward the cabin. All this in black silhouette against the silver moonlight.

Pain and my sickness were taking their toll on my eyesight again.

Not until the rider was very close to the door, just now getting his carbine ready, did I realize it was not Reeves at all, but Hollister, who must have doubled back and let the rest of the posse continue on. Good lawman that he was, he'd known that I couldn't leave without seeing Gillian and Annie one more time.

Now I knew how I'd get Annie taken care of.

I pressed back against the wall and let Hollister come through the door. Soft jingle of spur, faint creak of holster leather, hard quick rasp of tobacco lungs, scent of cold wind on his dark uniform.

He got four steps in and saw Annie where I'd rested her on the floor and then said, "My God!"

And set his carbine down on the kitchen table.

And rushed to little Annie. And knelt beside her. And lifted her head gently and tenderly upward so that he could see her face better. He no longer cared about his own safety—he knew I could be hiding anywhere in the cabin, but he didn't care. His overwhelming concern was Annie.

It's a funny thing about a man, how he can be crooked the way Hollister was with his prisoners when he was drunk, but be absolutely straight otherwise. Despite the animal he sometimes became in that little locked room of his in the police station, he held in his heart love and pity and duty, and I was watching all three at work now.

He rested Annie's head again and then started to stand up.

I stepped from the shadows, put my .45 on him.

"I want you to take her to the doc. Reeves brought his wolf out here. The wolf has rabies." I paused, wondering if I could actually say it out loud. "And so do I."

"Rabies!" he said. "You sure about that?"

"Yeah, I'm sure. That's why I've been so sick the last few days. One day I went out to Reeves' and the wolf bit me. There's a shot the doc can give her. You need to get her there now, and fast."

"But what about you? Won't you need the shot?"

"It's too late for me. All I'm worried about is Annie here."

We stood in the shifting darkness of the big front room, wind like ghosts whistling through the front door, fire guttering in the far grate.

"That posse'll find some way to kill you, Chase, if they ever catch up with you."

"I know."

"Why don't you come in with me?"

"I want to finish my business with Reeves."

"You keep mentioning Reeves. What the hell's he got to do with this?"

So I gave him a quick history.

"I'll be damned," he said.

"I just want you to get Annie to the doc."

"All right." Then he looked around. "Where's your wife?"

"Bedroom. You don't want to see her."

"The wolf?"

"Yeah."

"I'm sorry, Chase."

"Help me with Annie."

We bundled her in blankets and carried her out in the moonlight to Hollister's horse. He got up first and got himself ready, and then I handed her up. He cradled her across his saddle.

"She's a sweet little girl, Chase."

"She sure is."

"I'll get her to the doc right away."

"Wait here."

I went to the pines where I'd been hiding and got the money and brought it back and then tied the cord to Hollister's saddle horn.

"There's the bank money," I said.

"You're a pretty hard guy to figure out, Chase."

"Look who's talking."

He smiled. "I guess you're right."

I reached up and touched Annie's leg and stood there for a long moment with tears in my throat and a silent prayer on my lips.

And then Hollister was riding off, a dark shape against the moon-silver top of the hill, and then just receding hoofbeats in the night.

32

I took Gillian's horse.

In an hour I slid off the animal and started working my way to the poplars on the west side of Reeves' mansion. There would be an armed guard in those poplars.

The fever was getting worse. Every few minutes my vision would black out again and I'd feel a spasm of ice travel down my back and into my buttocks and legs. Then the dehydration would fix my tongue to the roof of my mouth.

The frost gave the land a fuzzy look, as if a silver moss had suddenly grown over everything. The stuff was cold on the palms of my hands, and when the fever got especially bad, I'd stop and put a cooling hand to my cheek.

From the size of him, I knew the man on duty had to be Hanratty. Reeves probably knew I was coming, so he put his best man on the job. Hanratty had likely been sleeping down in the bunkhouse when Reeves had roused him. Hanratty was day guard, not night guard.

He didn't hear me till I was close, too close, and just as he turned, I brought the butt of the carbine down against the side of his head.

He managed to swear and to glare at me, but then he sank in sections to the ground. I had nothing against Hanratty, but I wanted to make sure he didn't wake up and follow me into the house. I kicked him in the side of the head. He'd be out a long time but eventually he'd wake up. He was luckier than Gillian had been.

The first thing I wanted a look at was the wolf's cage.

I crept around the edge of the sweet-smelling jack pines for a good look. The cage was empty, its door flung wide.

The wolf was inside with Reeves.

I slipped through the shadows to the Victorian estate house. In the moonlight the cupolas and captain's walk had an exotic aspect, troubling the plain line of prairie and the jagged, barren stretch of mountains beyond, too fancy by half for such a landscape.

I was two steps from the front porch when I saw the man step from the shadows around the doorway.

The tip of his .45 glinted in the moonlight.

I put two bullets into him with my pistol before he could fire even once.

The noise was raucous in the vast prairie silence. The smell of gun smoke filled my nostrils.

Inside, in addition to the wolf, Reeves would have one, maybe two more men. And because of the gunfire, they now knew I was here.

I went around back, dropping to my knees halfway when blackness rushed up and knocked me down. The chills kept getting worse. I threw up, scared halfway through that I was going to choke on my own vomit. Panic . . .

When I was on my feet again, I reached the wide porch that ran the entire length of the rear.

The guard posted there wasn't very good. He was smoking a cigarette and the fire end made an easy target.

I put two shots into his face.

He made a grunting sound and fell facedown on to the porch.

I crouched, moving over to the porch door, got it open and then half crawled up the three steps.

Ahead of me lay the darkened kitchen door. Beyond that waited Reeves. . . .

On my way across the porch, I nudged a chair. The scraping noise could be heard clearly in the silence. The men inside would be able to chart every step of my progress.

I eased the kitchen door open. The scent of beef and spices filled the air.

Three more steps up and I stood in the kitchen. It was long and wide, with a fancy new ice box that stood out even in the gloom.

I got four steps across the linoleum floor when the gunny appeared in the archway leading to the dining room and shot me dead-on in the shoulder.

Pain joined my sickness and spun me around entirely. But as I was spinning I knew enough to put a shot of my own into him. I got him in the stomach.

I beat him with my fists until I knew he was dead. I'd actually done him a favor. Dying gut-shot was an experience nobody should have to go through.

Only as I started walking again did I realize how badly I was bleeding from my shoulder. I almost had to smile. There was so little left of me. The sickness had taken most of me; the gunshot claimed what remained.

I had just enough life left to finish what I needed to finish. . . .

When I got to the bottom of the staircase, my footsteps hollow on the parquet floor, I heard the wolf.

He was crying, and his cry was very much like my

own. But that wasn't surprising. We were both dying of the same disease.

I started up the sweeping staircase, grasping my weapon tight in my hand. With the shoulder in such sudden pain, I had to hold my gun very tight.

I reached the landing and stopped, staring up into the gloom above me. No lights shone; not even moonlight lent highlights to the darkness. Reeves had drawn all the heavy curtains.

I started up the remaining six steps. . . .

One, two, three steps, each one an agony for a man in my condition, my legs feeling as if they were weighted down by massive invisible boulders . . .

The gunshot flared against the shadows, there was even a certain beauty to it.

I threw myself on the stairs. The bullet ripped into the wainscoting behind me.

Four, five, six rifle shots cracked and roared and echoed down the sweeping stairway.

All I could do was lie there and listen to them, and listen to the wolf crying all the time.

I tried to remember how much I hated the beast for what he'd done to my brother and to my wife and daughter. And yet no matter how much I hated him, I hated Reeves even more, for what he'd trained the wolf to become.

I started crawling on my belly up the stairs. I didn't have much strength left. I needed to spend it while there was still time.

When I reached the top step, still lying flat, I raised my head an inch and stared deep into the gloom.

Reeves was crouched beneath a large gilt-framed painting of himself. A very aristocratic pose, that one.

Next to him crouched the wolf, eyes yellow in the

darkness, the cry still in its throat, forlorn as the cry of a wolf lost in a blizzard some prairie midnight.

Reeves saw me peeking up over the stairs and squeezed off several more shots. Apparently he had two or three rifles with him. He wouldn't need to reload for a while.

A silence, then, as I lay on the stairs, my body trembling from the chill, my throat constricted for want of water.

And then a whisper, a word of Indian I did not understand, the same word used that night when the wolf attacked me in my brother's room.

And then I heard the wolf, his paws scratching the floor as he began to pad over to the top of the stairs, a deep, chesty sound coming from him.

I raised my eyes and looked up directly into his as he lowered his blood-spattered head and prepared to lunge at me. He was still bleeding from the bullets Annie had put in him.

I slowly raised myself to my feet, sighting the .45 on his chest.

And he dove at me, all slashing teeth and furious noise.

He knocked me backward down the steps. My gun had fallen from my hands. I could defend my throat only by keeping my arms folded over my face.

Meanwhile we tumbled over and over down the stairs.

When we reached the landing, he renewed his attack, ripping flesh from my forearms so he could weaken me further and reach my throat. His teeth cut so deep that soon he was gnawing on raw bone. . . .

I was in the kind of delirium—fever, pain, fear, rage— a kind of dream state in which I functioned automatically.

Perhaps this was hell . . . a battle with the beast lasting for all eternity.

And then I remembered the knife I'd taken from our cottage. The bone-handled bowie . . .

Reaching it would mean that I would have to take one of my arms from my face . . . but there was little choice.

I started rolling across the landing, trying to confuse the wolf, trying to keep him from my throat. He kept crying and biting and hurling himself at me—

And as I rolled, I found the bone handle of the knife and yanked the blade free, and as I rolled over once again and saw the beast ready to spring—

I held the blade of the bowie knife up so that when he lunged—

He came in with his head down, teeth bared, spittle and blood flying from his mouth—came in so that he impaled himself on the blade.

It went straight and deep into his chest, and for a moment in his fury he did not allow himself to feel the wound—

He just kept trying to get at my throat, to rend and rip it open so that I would look like poor Gillian there on the bed.

But then the pain of the knife I kept pushing deeper and deeper into his chest finally registered—

And he stood on top of me, hot splashing blood beginning to flow from his wound, and he began to cry so loud and so sad in the gloom that I had no choice but to pity him. He cried his wolf song of cold icy waters and long lonely hunts; of seeing brothers and sisters die in bitter winter; of finding a moonlit pond in a midnight forest and sleeping peacefully there; of finding a mate strong enough to follow him into the mountains and bear the offspring who would make them both so proud—sadness and grief and joy and pride, all that and much more in wolf song as the beast stood upon me and I in my pain and sickness and weakness and curious final strength watched as Reeves descended the stairs, wanting to finish me off since his trained wolf could no longer do the job himself.

But when he was halfway down the stairs, Reeves in his fancy ruffled shirt and expensive dark suit, his rifle aimed directly at my heart—when he was about to kill me, the wolf turned abruptly and sprang on him and proceeded to tear and rend in a frenzy so loud and vicious I wanted to cover my eyes.

All I could hear was Reeves screaming and screaming and screaming there in the moonlight of the stair landing. . . .

And when the wolf was finished, he came back and lay next to me, and took up his crying once more.

In some way we are brothers, this wolf and I, lying here dying as the cold dark winds of November whip through this now-useless mansion. . . .

His cry is even louder now, and I wish I could comfort him, but there is no comfort for either of . . .

. . . not for a few minutes yet . . .

. . . not until the darkness.

It is a sunny afternoon and Gillian and Annie are coming toward me on the bicycle, Annie on the handlebars, golden hair glowing.

And then it is dark and I am looking down at my dead brother in the bed that night and I am wanting to cry.

And then there is a barn dance and Gillian looks so beautiful in the autumn night and—

And then my mother is there, plain prairie woman, plain prairie wisdom evident in her kind gaze, and she puts out her hand so I will not be afraid in these last moments.

Dreams, phantasms, memory . . . all memory dying with me now . . .

Gillian—
Annie—

And finally the darkness
the wolf and I
and the   darkness.